THE BALD HILLS

Douglas City was a peaceful, isolated community, nearly cut off from the rest of the world. Until the hard-faced stranger appeared, the only real problem was to get the cattle from the Bald Hills to a market where they could be sold to raise cash.

But after that dark, unfriendly stranger, other riders appeared out of the trackless mountains. Then the stranger was shot to death in a gunfight.

But that was only the beginning.

Lauran Paine who, under his own name and various pseudonyms has written over 900 books, was born in Duluth, Minnesota, a descendant of the Revolutionary War patriot and author, Thomas Paine. His family moved to California when he was at an early age and his apprenticeship as a Western writer came about through the years he spent in the livestock trade, rodeos, and even motion pictures where he served as an extra because of his expert horsemanship in several films starring movie cowboy Johnny Mack Brown. In the late 1930s, Paine trapped wild horses in Northern Arizona and even, for a time, worked as a professional farrier. Paine came to know the Old West through the eyes of many who had been born in the previous century and he learned that Western life had been very different from the way it was portrayed on the screen. "I knew men who had killed other men," he later recalled. "But they were the exceptions. Prior to and during the Depression, people were just too busy eking out an existence to indulge in Saturday-night brawls." He served in the U.S. Navy in the Second World War and began writing for Western pulp magazines following his discharge. It is interesting to note that all of his earliest novels (written under his own name and the pseudonym Mark Carrel) were published in the British market and he soon had as strong a following in that country as in the United States. Paine's Western fiction is characterized by strong plots, authenticity, an apparently effortless ability to construct situation and character, and a preference for building his stories upon a solid foundation of historical fact. *Adobe Empire* (1956), one of his best novels, is a fictionalized account of the last twenty years in the life of trader William Bent and, in an off-trail way, has a melancholy, bittersweet texture that is not easily forgotten. *Moon Prairie* (1950), first published in the United States in 1994, is a memorable story set during the mountain man period of the frontier. In later novels such as *The Homesteaders* (1986) or *The Open Range Men* (1990), he showed that the special magic and power of his stories and characters had only matured along with his basic themes of changing times, changing attitudes, learning from experience, respecting nature, and the yearning for a simpler, more moderate way of life. His most recent Western novels include *Tears of the Heart*, *Lockwood* and *The White Bird*.

THE BALD HILLS

Lauran Paine

GUNSMOKE

This hardback edition 2002
by Chivers Press
by arrangement with
Golden West Literary Agency

ISBN 0 7540 8171 0

British Library Cataloguing in Publication Data available.

Printed and bound in Great Britain by
BOOKCRAFT, Midsomer Norton, Somerset

Chapter One

The rivers were grand and deep. The mountains awesome, broad and massive. There stood shaggy-barked redwoods so huge they couldn't be girdled by just one lariat rope; they were older than any other living thing.

It was a wild, brooding, majestic world apart from every area; cut off from the San Joaquin Valley by trackless forest and tiers of purple mountains. Southward, by following down the ocean coastline lay civilization, and northward, up that same stretch of grey sand and stone, was Oregon. It was a huge cemetery of forlorn hopes peopled by men and women who were alternately deafened by a pounding surf, or made breathless by the kind of forest-silence that turns people inward with their awed listenings.

But it had the Bald Hills, some of the finest graze in the world. Green year round because of the warm coastal rains in summertime, green in the winter for the same reason. It was not a hot place, but neither was it ever really cold. Damp occasionally, yes, but otherwise very livable, very rich, very productive—and very lonely.

There were remnants of Indian groups in the forests. Sometimes they came out into the Bald Hills country too, in their endless quest for game. Sometimes too, they didn't hunt deer, elk, pheasant, quail, or the grubs they worked up into a palatable—to them—paste, because fat cattle were a very great temptation.

There was a sort of unwritten concordant among the cowmen: Don't shoot an Indian who is stealing a beef. It is much cheaper to feed them now and then, and otherwise they fill animals full of arrows out of spite, the

5

loss is much greater, and there is danger that they'll also kill cowmen and townsmen.

This made a sort of truce workable in the Bald Hills country. The redmen still shot an occasional traveller for his horse, his clothing, his weapons, but even this was better, so the cowmen insisted, than setting out to punish them, and getting ambushed in forests no white man would ever know as well as the redmen did.

The Bald Hills lay in Humboldt County of far Northern California; cut off, insular, uninformed and unendingly the same. Several of the coastal towns had wharves. This was how all trade was conducted for many years. If the ships came to take off cattle in their holds and bring in supplies, the economy was healthy. When high seas ran, the ships didn't try making the schedule, the economy suffered.

None of it was very complicated; neither the economy, the existence, the weather, nor the endless miles of the Bald Hills which rose and fell, rose and fell, treeless knobs covered with grass ideal for cattle and the men who owned the cattle.

When a stranger got off one of the ships, even though he might remain in town, he was still a novelty. If he went inland he was a downright curiosity, and the people of this hidden area, having little else to do, speculated endlessly on his past, his probable future, and his reason for being there.

It was the old story of an environment moulding its people; the natives were rarely very intelligent, and somehow had come to equate nosiness and gossiping ability with genuine intellect. Whoever knew the most or freshest gossip, was looked up to as being worth cultivating.

They weren't all that way, of course, but a good ninety-five per cent of them were. A stranger would be dissected piecemeal by people whose ignorance was colossal. Then he would be put back together again—incorrectly—and the assessments would be passed around as gospel truth.

All but one. He didn't come on the ships and where he stopped scarcely a soul knew he was in the country until he'd ridden the hill and river trails, learned the forest pathways becoming as familiar with them as someone born to the area. It may have been this familiarity that let this particular outlander almost slip through the native network of nosiness. But it was the very method of his arrival in the Bald Hills country that finally focused the interest upon him. He had come overland through the forests, down the blackly twisting canyons, and over the grey-hazed peaks—and he'd lived to get through it all. That made him unique. It also made him suspect.

In the town of Douglas—named for the variety of fir tree—Paul Standish told the other two men sitting in the saloon with him, that he felt uncomfortable around the stranger; felt downright uneasy even when they stood shoulder to shoulder at a bar, let alone going down a four-hundred-mile trail with him.

Cap Bozeman had one of his eminently practical replies to that statement. 'Keep him in front all the while. Pretty hard for a man to cause you grief when he's got his back to you up front, Paul. Besides; I think you just got it in for him. I been around him a time, an' he's always polite, quiet, and willin'.'

The third man was short, broad, built like a bull. He owned the saloon. He also owned a large tract of land and ran cattle on shares with two youths out there. His name was Phil Barker. He was an astute, tough individual who saw straight to the core of things brushing aside superfluities with a rough brusqueness.

'Paul,' he said shortly, looking straight at Standish. 'What choice we got?'

That was the crux of their problem in a nutshell. Each

of them knew it, too. Standish didn't answer. He reached for the beer glass in front of him and drank deeply. When he set the glass down he still didn't speak. There was no need, actually, since they had no alternative.

Phil Barker slapped the tabletop with his palm. 'Exactly,' he exclaimed, as though Standish had audibly agreed with Barker's train of thought. 'None. We got no choice. The stranger hires on to trail our cattle out and down into the San Joaquin country where the buyers are, or the lousy cattle stay in here and die of old age.'

John Bozeman said, 'Paul, I know you're a church-goin' man—you'n Annie—and I figure that's to your credit, of course, only sometimes church-goin' folks get pretty stiff-necked and mulish about what's right and what's wrong in this life. They figure Satan's behind all the evil. Well, he might be for all I know, but I can tell you one thing a man's learnt by the time he's fifty— what's evil now isn't necessarily evil tomorrow; what looks wrong to you, don't look wrong to me at all.'

Standish was a large, grave man, younger than the grey above his ears made him look. He had one of those long, lipless mouths that ordinarily stamped a bigot. His eyes were light brown and unsmiling. He put them on Cap Bozeman as he said, 'John; I have a feeling about that stranger. I told you that.'

Bozeman's faded blue eyes ironically twinkled. 'Sure you have,' he quietly said. 'But the point I'm tryin' to get across to you, is that as far as we three are concerned, we shouldn't give a damn. All we want is for him to take the combined herd out. That's all. He knows the way, and we don't. We're just hiring a guide, that's all. We're not goin' to make him mayor or sheriff or senator. Just a trail-boss on a trail-drive. You understand, Paul; we don't give a damn if he's wanted somewhere—which I'll admit is possible—because it's *our* future we're lookin' to, not *his* past.'

8

This struck Phil Barker just right. He brought his palm down upon the tabletop again, vigorously nodding approval of Cap John Bozeman's words.

The options left to Paul Standish were obvious; go along with the thinking of the other two or drop out. Phil squirmed and flagged the barman for a refill of his beer glass. He needed the money those cattle would fetch. Like the others, he'd been operating half a year on promises that as soon as the ships came and he sent cattle southward again, he'd pay all his debts. The ships hadn't come; he couldn't go on promises a whole lot longer, hence he really had no alternative at all and he knew it.

The barman brought a pitcher of beer, set it squarely in front of the three men and returned behind his bar again to continue an interrupted conversation with a couple of rangeriders over there. A battered Seth Thomas clock over the back-bar placidly ticked, while outside in the dust and sunshine people passed back and forth going about their business.

Cap Bozeman poured the glasses full, hoisted his and drank deeply, appreciatively. He afterwards sucked both ends of his bushy, drooping Longhorn moustache, and wiped the foam out of it. He was watching Paul Standish. John Bozeman had been in the war many years ago; he knew men. He was a thoughtful bachelor with a nose for making money. He was lanky, slow-moving, amiable and at the same time quietly reserved. He was a patient man too, which showed now as the three of them sat hunched around their pitcher of beer in dour silence.

Eventually he said, 'Paul; I reckon Annie won't approve, but every now an' then folks got to compromise or go under. You're not makin' any big concession to your principles anyway. All you're doin' is figurin' a way to keep your head above water. We're all in the same boat.'

9

Standish looked straight at Cap Bozeman. 'And suppose he makes off with our cattle, Cap, or suppose he gets the money and heads on over the Sierras somewhere?'

'He won't get the money because it'll be sent back to us in San Francisco bank drafts which he couldn't convert to currency,' stated Phil Barker. 'That's our guarantee for this part of it. And if he wants to go on over the mountains after he finishes the drive for us—that'll be all right with me—providin' he finishes the drive first.'

Standish had his back to the wall. He said, 'Speaking of guarantees, how do we know he'll agree to head up the drive?'

Cap smiled gently. 'That's something we'll have to find out from him; the thing we're doin' right now is agreein' he's the man for the job. If we're agreed on that now, why then the next step is to talk to him.' Cap felt through his pockets for a cigar and lit it. Cigars were a genuine luxury; they came on the ships from far southward, were inordinately expensive, and only a very few men could afford them. Usually, only the single men.

Phil Barker was getting impatient. He set his square jaw and turned his hard, tough gaze on Paul Standish ready to demand a forthright answer. Standish could feel that, apparently, or see it in Barker's face. He nodded his head. 'All right. It's a squeeze though. I'm still against the man, at least until we hear more about him. But I'll throw in.'

Bozeman drifted fragrant smoke ceilingward. 'Be careful what you believe about him, Paul; in this country you can hear anything about anyone. Maybe some day we'll get newspapers and books in here. Then folks won't have to manufacture so much malicious gossip about one another. But the way it stands right now, this stranger's got more stories bein' spun about him than you can shake a stick at.'

10

Standish suddenly said, 'Cap; do you like his looks?'

Bozeman's grin deepened. 'I wonder what he'd say if I asked him the same question about you, Paul. Or Phil here. Or me, for that matter. Like his looks? Well; I don't *dislike* 'em. I've seen enough men who wore guns to tell you one thing—don't pick no fight with him.'

Standish reached for his glass registering disapproval in every movement. Phil Barker looked around his log saloon and back again. 'Now that it's settled,' he told them. 'I'll nail him first time he rides in, and put the proposition to him. If he agrees, fine. If he doesn't agree . . .' Barker shrugged heavy shoulders. 'We're right back where we were—only worse.' He arose from the table and went down the room where several men who had just entered the log building were lining up at his bar.

Cap smoked, watched Paul Standish with an ironic twinkle in his eye, and sat all loose and easy in his chair as though he didn't have a worry in the world, which was the privilege of bachelors because actually, they didn't have, even though they might be in a financial squeeze such as the one Bozeman was in now. There was no need to plan for a prolonged future, nor to scheme ways to leave wealth to another generation, for men like John Bozeman, and he was realist enough to know that. Life was an interesting game to such men; it could end tomorrow and they might smile softly with small regret, but they had no cause for worry about a future that had never belonged to them anyway. In a lot of ways it was the ideal existence for a man.

'Tell Annie,' he said to Paul Standish, 'you're not giving approval to the stranger. You're only using a man. That's all. Just using his knowledge of the passes and trails, and there's the end of it.' Cap couldn't resist a little jibe though, because like most men whose lives had run the gamut, he didn't have much use for organized religion. 'If she doesn't like it, Paul, tell her to pray for some other solution.'

Standish's light-dark eyes lifted, sternly, then he arose and left Cap, the table and the remains of their pitcher of beer, strode out of the saloon into the pleasant day beyond.

Chapter Two

As a town Douglas wasn't much, but as a setting for a town there was a lot in its favour. There were mountains in the distant background, the Pacific Ocean wasn't very many miles westward. Elsewhere close by, were broad savannahs—called prairies or plains—and the lift and fall of the Bald Hills, green ten months out of the year.

The only serious objection, aside from its remoteness, to the town of Douglas, was that during wintertime's rainy season there was fog. It got so thick sometimes a man on horseback could get completely lost within a mile of his home. Of course the people knew when to expect this blight, knew how to live with it, and except for the annoyance, they were more or less passive about their shrouding fogs.

In Douglas it was less a problem, when it came, than it was on the ranges; Douglas wasn't a large place, people could step into stores and get re-oriented without difficulty. But the fog didn't come during summertime. Rains did though, softly warm and gentle, a natural blessing people welcomed because the rains kept their garden plots thriving, kept the grasslands strong with rich feed for livestock, and always washed the air clean of dust and pollen.

Douglas sat near the upper end of a broad valley which began down where the greenish surf pounded giant rocks. It was a log town because logs were plentiful and free. Phil Barker's saloon—called unimaginatively *The Douglas Saloon*—was on the south side of a very broad roadway. Opposite it stood a general store, while next to the saloon was the harness works and saddlery.

Douglas had a café, a barber shop complete with elegant striped pole out front brought north on one of the ships at considerable expense to the bald barber. Douglas also had a number of other business ventures on both sides of that wide thoroughfare, and at the south end of town, in fact some little distance below town, were a network of large holding-corrals. Here was where the cattle were brought and held until a drive was made up, then they were drifted down the flat, loamy coastline between mountains and ocean, to the distant, larger communities that had wharves for the cattle boats.

In most ways Douglas was a picturesque place, peaceful, substantial, not old, really, but with an appearance of age because of those thick, dark log structures. Commerce in Douglas City had a leisurely pace; the people were frugal spenders, except for the rangemen, and they were the same as all rangemen everywhere; young footloose, hard-working and hard-spending. The trouble now was that since they hadn't been paid in several months—since after the last boats had come north to take away the cattle—they didn't liven things up in town, particularly on Saturday nights, the way they normally did.

Sheriff Murphy Crail didn't mind this respite. He was a large, powerful man with age settling in around his middle, who was perfectly capable of handling hoorawing cowboys, but he preferred things as they now were, peaceful and undisturbed.

Murphy was a pleasant man. He'd come to the Bald Hills country to work at logging, and for two years he'd followed that line of endeavour, but Murphy Crail wasn't a very motivated man; he'd sweat when he couldn't avoid it, and he'd fight a lion the same way—if he had to—but by nature big stolid Murphy Crail was lazy. He knew the stranger; at least he knew him by sight; had once exchanged bought-beers with him, and because he made

14

a habit of shying clear of the implications in all the local gossip, he let the stranger strictly alone.

There were undoubtedly men in the Bald Hills country who had left unpleasant pasts somewhere down country or inland, but as long as they behaved themselves Murph Crail was no threat to them.

The morning Annie Standish cornered Murph outside the general store with some pointed questions about the stranger, Murph made what would have been called elsewhere his 'policy statement'. He said the stranger minded his own business, bothered no one, paid his debts and caused no trouble. And that if he was wanted somewhere, why then, until that fact was brought to Sheriff Crail's attention—and proved beyond a reasonable doubt—Murph wasn't going to go prying around the man.

It seemed Cap Bozeman had summed it up well enough when he'd told Paul Standish what mattered about the stranger wasn't what he might have been elsewhere, but what he actually now was in the Bald Hills country. Annie threw her head in the air and walked stiffly away from Murph Crail, that morning, to report to Paul that in her opinion Sheriff Crail was a lazy no-good ex-logger with jelly for a backbone.

If that were true, then it had to be fairly substantial jelly; you couldn't hang a two-hundred-and-twenty-pound frame on just any kind of jelly, nor hold it together where the muscles bulged like hawsers, either, which was the way Murphy Crail was built.

And if Murph lacked forceful thrust, it was just as well. Otherwise frustration might have driven him to drink because there was so little real trouble in his territory a more dedicated lawman would have been forced to find some other release for his energies.

Murph made his rounds, not only of the town, but of the countryside, when the spirit moved him. Because of

15

his size he rode a big grey horse weighing over a thousand pounds who couldn't turn fast nor move speedily, but then Murph was no cowboy anyway; all he needed was great strength and durability, and the grey horse had both.

The day he left town heading up into the north-westerly fringes of the Bald Hills on one of his periodic forays, Phil Barker, standing out front his saloon with Abe Sherman the blacksmith, watched him leave town with a wry comment. 'When Murph ties up outside the house for his noon meal, the rancher's wife wherever he stops will have to fry up another five steaks and boil up another five pounds of spuds.'

Abe Sherman, with his close-cropped dark beard and bushy brows, was the town wag. Abe, like a great proportion of the locals, was a bachelor. He delighted in practical jokes. Now, stroking his furry jowls and also watching Murph head into the back country, he said, 'I got a chair I been workin' on down at the shop. It's built so's the legs collapse. When I get it finished I'll fetch it up and put it at his favourite table in your saloon. Phil. Then we'll get a laugh when Murph sits down.'

Sometimes Abe's stunts came close to causing blows, like the time he managed to slip two cut-outs from a racy magazine into Paul Standish's coat pocket in church. But that time the reason there were no blows was because Abe had discreetly gone fishing for the balance of the day, Paul couldn't find him, and Annie said she knew perfectly well someone had played a prank on her man; that Paul Standish wouldn't even look at pictures like that, let alone carry them around with him.

But Paul nevertheless remained cool towards Abe for the balance of that winter. The trouble was, though, Abe was the only blacksmith; he was somewhat like a doctor in the Bald Hills country; eventually Paul Standish'd had to go to him for horseshoes, and after that Paul watched

Abe like a hawk, but was civil.

The Douglas City church was a log house built by volunteer labour. It had no ordained minister, only lay preachers who alternated at the pulpit. Like the Douglas City jailhouse, it had been constructed of huge, square-adzed logs knocked into place so tightly no mud filler was needed between them. It sat near the lower, or westerly, end of town and had a wrought-iron cross atop it, donated by Abe Sherman, who wasn't a punctual parishioner, but who did nevertheless show up occasionally, the same as did nearly everyone else. The best way to win approval in Douglas City was to attend Sunday services, and that was another thing that went against the stranger. He'd never once ridden into town on a Sunday. Not to attend church services, nor even, in the afternoon when Barker's bar was opened for business, to have a drink or two.

Cap Bozeman had a theory about that which he explained to Martin Leffler, the general store proprietor, one evening over a game of chequers out front of the rooming-house where they both lived. 'Some men are just naturally loners, Martin. You know how that works. A man gets used to being alone; he gets so's he's downright uncomfortable being around crowds. This feller came through the mountains alone. Maybe before that, he lived alone too. But whether that's so or not, I can tell you from experience, he's just not built for towns and crowds of people. My notion about men like that goes back to war; I've seen 'em change almost overnight. They get so's they don't trust the world. Don't like human company as well as animal company. Not bitter, mind you, just detached. Just—different.'

Leffler, who was bald and portly and sharp-eyed, said, 'I've sold him tobacco and tinned goods a time or two. You want to know my opinion, Cap? He's some kind of gunfighter. At least he *has* been. He's got that look to

17

him. He's quiet and tall and moves easy, like a mountain lion.'

'Well hell, Martin; he's not more'n twenty-five or thirty. When you were that young you moved easy too.'

'Did I wear a pistol with an ivory butt, or keep my holster thonged to my leg like he does? Did I come along and mingle with folks and never even tell 'em my name? No; this one's trouble. Maybe not to us in Douglas, but somewhere he's been in trouble.'

They played their game for a while in the settling dusk of a pleasantly warm evening, then Cap said, 'I'll bet you a dollar that's where Murph went this morning; up into the Bald Hills to look him up and visit with him.'

'Murph,' snorted Martin Leffler, 'couldn't pry the plain truth out of a blabber-mouth an' you know it. He won't get a damned thing out of the stranger.'

'A man don't always have to tell you things, Martin, if you've got eyes in your head. The way he lives, eats, moves, looks, can tell you an awful lot about a man.'

'Except his name.'

Cap jumped two of Leffler's men and smiled 'A name only lets you know one man from another. It's not very important. You can change names as often as you change your drop-seat underwear, Martin. I never went much on names. You recall President Grant's brother Orville? Well; he had a good name, but that didn't stop him from being tried for underhandedly dealing in Indian-Agency supplies, dit it?'

Martin didn't answer. He'd made another tomfool move and Cap corralled another of his chequers. All he said was, 'Damnation.'

Smoke rose above Douglas City, fragrant, bluish-tinted curling against the advancing evening. Most folks were indoors for supper; only Cap Bozeman, Martin Leffler and one or two others saw the unshaven, dark-faced man guide his horse down into Douglas City from out of the shadowy northwesterly hills. He was a stranger to everyone who saw him arrive in town. Moreover, he had a familiar appearance; not a personal look of familiarity, but a general look of it. He had a tied-down gun on his hip, a carbine slung forward with the butt-plate tipped up for easy access. His boots and spurs, even his saddle and horse, looked typical.

Martin Leffler watched the solitary rider pass the full length of the wide roadway, then said in a low whisper, 'If I hadn't seen his face was different, Cap, I'd swear he was the stranger.'

'*A* stranger,' corrected Cap. 'But there's sure-enough a sameness, isn't there? Now I wonder where he came from?'

'You saw,' exclaimed Leffler, leaning to watch the newcomer head into the liverybarn. 'He came from the back-country.'

Cap nodded, steadily looking down there where the newcomer had disappeared. 'Sure did, didn't he? That's the second one to reach Douglas from through the mountains.'

'Yes, and I don't like it either. This one looks just as dangerous as the other one, Cap.'

But Bozeman's thoughts were on a different tangent. 'He'd know the trails through also. He'd know how to get a herd down into the San Joaquin. Now this gives us something to work with; we won't be beholden to just one man.'

Leffler leaned back. The stranger emerged from the barn, paused out there in the night to look up and down, then stepped to the public trough, hung his hat from the pump handle and proceeded to wash. He was a thick-shouldered, narrow-hipped man with black hair, dark skin, and sinewy arms. When he was finished he mopped off surplus water, dumped the wide-brimmed hat back atop his head and slowly, methodically made a cigarette. In the harsh flare of the match his face looked lined, lean, and tired. It also looked as though this man hadn't smiled in a very long while.

The liveryman sauntered forth, said something and pointed over towards the rooming-house. He also pointed up where lamplight shone from the café window. The newcomer nodded and walked towards the restaurant, smoke trailing over one shoulder in the warm night.

Martin Leffler and Cap Bozeman watched the stranger's long stride, the easy, supple swing of his body. When the man halted outside the window of the café and looked in, making a close study of the counter and their occupants and the caféman, before reaching to open the door and enter, Leffler said, sounding bitterly pleased with himself. 'Well; you were right, Cap. A man's actions do reveal a sight more'n his name. Did you see how he made certain of who was inside before he opened the door?'

'Of course I saw it, Martin.'

'Well; what kind of man moves in the dark lookin' through windows, except an outlaw, or someone—'

'Oh hell, Martin,' muttered Cap, fishing for one of his stogies. 'He just wanted to make sure the place wasn't too crowded.'

Leffler's brows shot straight up. 'Here? In Douglas City, the café too crowded?'

Cap lit a cigar, killed the fire and leaned back in his porch chair, saying nothing more. He had a speculative, keen and alert expression upon his face. There were thoughts moving in Cap Bozeman's mind he didn't seem to wish to share with the storekeeper. He rocked and smoked and kept watching the orange-lighted café window across the road.

Douglas City had its ingrained habits. After supper

20

folks retired, usually, or perhaps strolled the night. The town was quiet. Even at the *Douglas Saloon* there wasn't much noise although there were always patrons at the bar. Saddle animals drowsed out front, lights burned cheerily, and men talked of the mandatory trail-drive, and drank in a pleasant atmosphere.

Chapter Three

Sheriff Crail didn't return to town until the following morning, which was natural. He'd bedded down at one of the ranches against the Bald Hills and had taken his time both going and coming. He had no reason not to. Even when he put up his horse at the liverybarn and was at once informed about the stranger, Murph still wasn't at all anxious. Curious, yes, but not worried. It wasn't impossible to come through the purple mountains; the original founders of Douglas City had come overland that way.

'But,' exclaimed Martin Leffler when Murph came in for a sack of Bull Durham and stopped long enough to speak his mind about this newcomer, 'you got to admit, Murphy, it's unusual.'

Murph didn't admit anything. He tore open the sack, built himself a lumpy smoke and lit up. He'd run out of smokes the day before; it had been an uncomfortable interim for him. As the nicotine went to work, he said, 'He's gone anyway, Martin.'

'Gone? What d'you mean gone? Cap and I saw him ride in last night, eat his supper, then walk right past us on the porch to engage a room for the night at the—'

'Martin; I don't care about all that,' said Murphy Crail. 'He's gone. Took his horse out about sun-up and rode off. The liveryman showed me where he'd put the man's horse.'

Martin Leffler turned thoughtful. He leaned his paunch upon the counter and propped his head in one hand. 'I'll bet you a dollar he went up to where that other one is, north of the Bald Hills.'

Murph licked his cigarette where the paper was coming loose. 'You just lost a damned dollar,' he mumbled, examining the mended cigarette. 'The other one's gone.'

Leffler's eyes got perfectly round. 'Gone . . .?'

'Yup. I went up to set a spell with him. He's gone. His camp's struck. All that's left is the stone ring for his cookin' fire, the peeled limbs of the tree he lived under where he hung stuff, and that little saplin' corral he made for his horse.'

Leffler studied this over for a long while before advancing his thoughts again. 'All right. Then I'll bet you a dollar *that* one knew *this* one was coming, and pulled stakes because the one who come into town last night is lookin' for the other one.'

Murph looked pained. 'That's pretty complicated,' he muttered. 'Anyway; what difference does it make as long as whatever they do, isn't done around here an' isn't against the law?'

Paul Standish walked in, gazed at the storekeeper and sheriff, then crossed to where they were standing alone in the store. 'Either of you seen Cap?' he asked. They shook their heads, but Leffler suggested that Bozeman would be around some time in the day. Standish's light-brown eyes were troubled. 'I'll go hunt him up,' he muttered. 'We can't get that cattle drive started after all.'

'Why not?' queried Leffler, to whom Standish and all the other cowmen owed sizeable accounts.

'We talked about hiring that stranger who's camped up in the Bald Hills to trail-boss the outfit through into the San Joaquin.' Standish shook his head. 'I just talked to him. He refused.'

Murphy Crail's eyes brightened perceptibly. 'Where did you just talk to him, Paul?'

'Over at the saloon,' said Standish, and walked away.

23

Leffler leered. 'Struck his camp and disappeared, did he?'

Murph reddened. 'I never said he disappeared. I only said—oh, go to hell, Martin.'

Outside, the morning had a sultry, summertime fragrance to it, rich with the scent of pines and junipers, wild flowers and warm, mouldy earth. Up in front of the *Douglas Saloon* a saddlehorse with a blanket-roll aft of the cantle, wrapped in a waterproof piece of heavy cloth, stood comfortably alone. There weren't many people abroad. Sunlight lay golden and bright throughout the town, and even managed to lighten the sombre hues of the faraway hills. It was not the kind of morning Murph Crail—or anyone else for that matter—would have expected trouble to erupt. As a matter of fact, trouble usually came in the night; at least in the hot afternoon. It just didn't belong in a scented, warm and golden morning such as this one was.

Abe Sherman was sweating a steel tyre onto a wagon wheel, which was a meticulous undertaking requiring all the blacksmith's attention; the tyre had to be sized perfectly and hot enough to be expanded but not hot enough to char the felloes or warp the spokes. It had to be dunked properly in the huge circular tub, also, which cooled the steel to form a perfect bond between alien parts, metal and wood, otherwise, when the wood shrunk in hot weather, the tyre would simply fall off.

At the liverybarn a hostler was dunging stalls, a chore requiring not nearly as much knowledgeable concentration, but then the hostler wasn't capable of knowledgeable concentration anyway, so even this routine job occupied all his attention.

Only Phil Barker, behind his bar, had any inkling things weren't right, and except for the quiet, bronzed man leaning across his bar this morning, Phil was alone in his pungent establishment.

24

The Bald Hills

He served the rangerider a beer and a shot-glass of whiskey, privately wondering what kind of a breakfast that was for a man. He waited until his patron had downed both, then, while vigorously polishing a glass, said, 'Mister; I got a proposition for you.' The stranger didn't raise his face; he was toying with the empty little shot-glass. 'Three of us are going to pool herds. There'll be maybe fifteen hundred head in the bunch. We need someone to take them through the mountains down into the San Joaquin Valley where there are buyers. Normally, we ship by sea, but there aren't any ships and we've got to get some ready money.'

At last, the silent man raised his head. He was one of those old-young men with shadows in their eyes, a flat mouth and a straight nose. He could be a mean man, or just a taciturn one. But that ivory-butted, tied-down gun he wore suggested more the former than the latter.

He said, 'Why me, barman?'

Phil put aside the glass and towel. 'You came through the mountains.'

'Did I?'

Phil's neck reddened. 'Mister; unless folks come up the coast on ships to Douglas City an' the Bald Hills, they got to come through the mountains. That's no secret. All I'm sayin' is that you know how to get in here, so you'll know how to get out again—with a herd of cattle. We'll pay you a percentage of what the herd brings and furnish you with six cowboys.'

'Sounds fair enough,' drawled the younger, taller man. 'Except that I'm goin' back through those hills—alone.'

Phil reached for a whiskey bottle, filled the shot-glass, put the bottle aside and leaned on his bar. 'Mister; you'd be doin' us a mighty big favour. Years back there were a few men around who knew the mountain trails. After the ships started comin', no one had to know how to reach the outside any other way. I doubt if there's a man left, even among the old ones, who could find his way through any more.'

'Thanks for the drink,' said the sun-darkened man, and downed his whiskey as he backed off the bar. 'Barman; anyone can find that trail. It's not marked but as long as a feller rides watchin' the skyline, he can pick the passes and head for them.' For a moment the stranger was contemplative, then he said, 'But fifteen hundred head of cattle ... It'd be quite a chore. Some of those damned canyons are deeper'n hell itself, and in other places you got to wind around rock ledges with eagles flyin' a mile down under you.'

'We'd make the percentage high enough to pay you for all the trouble. And we'd send along six of the best rangemen in the Bald Hills,' said Barker, watching that lean, hard face for some sign of weakening. 'Anything else you need—pack animals, grub, we'd furnish too.'

The stranger's heavy-lidded, hawk-like eyes fell upon Phil Barker, unblinking. 'How do you know ships won't come?' he asked. 'I've watched the ocean out there; it's mostly quiet now. While I don't know a blessed thing about ships—never even saw the ocean before I got through to Douglas City—I can't see why ships can't make it up here.'

'The point is,' explained Barker, 'we can't wait. We've already waited too long, hopin' they would come. We've got to sell cattle an' get working capital. Even if a ship came the day you left with the cattle, it still wouldn't help us now.'

'Why not?'

'Because a ship can only haul sixty to eighty head at a time.'

The stranger mulled that over, resettled the hat atop his head, glanced at himself in the back-bar mirror, then slowly wagged his head. 'Can't help you, barman.'

'If we pay you in advance—in gold?'

26

Those heavy-lidded eyes flicked down to Phil's face again. 'Not even then. I'm leavin' today. Thanks again for the drink.' The stranger turned and sauntered across and out of the saloon with Phil Barker watching his departure as though his last hope for survival went with that man. Then he pulled off his apron starting to rush around the bar and go after the stranger to make one last plea.

Phil reached the doors moving rapidly, and nearly ran right into his own demise. The stranger was out there in the golden sunlight beside the horse with the bedroll behind the saddle-cantle, one hand ready to free the animal from the tie rack, the other hand lightly atop the pole. Across the road was another saddled horse, out front of the general store. That animal showed signs of having just been ridden hard.

There was also a man over there, leaning on a post in soft-scented shade. He looked enough like the man Phil had just pleaded with to be his twin—almost. That one, in his shadowy place, called across the road, which was almost empty, his voice scarcely loud enough to carry.

'Froman!'

The rider in front of Phil jerked his head up, looking straight across the golden, empty roadway. Otherwise, he didn't move a muscle.

'Froman,' said the opposite man, straightening off that post. 'I got a message for you.'

Froman very slowly straightened up leaving his horse still tied to the pole. He looked astonished, to Phil, but then Barker couldn't really see his expression, only his profile. But Barker had a good view of the other one, the man across in front of Leffler's store, and he didn't look the least bit surprised; he looked deadly.

'I'll hand it to you, Froman, you sure picked the devil's own backyard to get lost in. But every man leaves tracks. One way or another, every man leaves his sign.'

27

The Bald Hills

Annie Standish walked out of the general store, saw both those men, and didn't even see what was going to happen. She tossed her head, set her back to them and went marching properly homeward with her purchases clasped in both hands.

Phil Barker knew exactly what was going to happen and wanted the worst way to move, but he didn't for the elemental reason that the first person to move within the perimeter of those two men, was going to precipitate a killing, and just might be the victim himself.

Froman eased his hands away from the tie-rack, eased his body half erect and stood studying the man over there in the shade. He knew him, there wasn't any question of that in Phil Barker's mind, and he was going to try to kill him.

'It's been a long trip,' said the man in front of Leffler's place. 'And now we're at the end of it—both of us. You have anything to say to me?'

Froman breathed deeply. Phil saw his shoulders and chest softly rise and fall. He dived for his gun. The second Froman moved, so did Phil; he dropped to the plankwalk. Those two guns sounded almost simultaneously. The man across the road barely seemed to move at all but behind him Leffler's glass window exploded into a thousand shattered shards. The man himself, standing like he was carved from stone, held his trigger flat and used his thumb to fire the pistol with. He raised and dropped his hammer three times.

Froman just fired twice. That first slug broke Leffler's window. The second bullet hit somewhere up along the high front of the store making a sound of solid impact. Then Froman reached for the tie-rack, missed it and fell to his knees. He dropped the gun and looked dumbly at his horse. The animal was setting back in terror but the rawhide reins held him fast.

The one of them still standing upright, then let go with

28

his third bullet. Phil was horrified; Froman was out of it. He'd dropped his gun even. He was kneeling down there in the sunlight like a man at his prayers, and the other stranger deliberately shot him the third time.

Froman dropped backwards, both legs curled awkwardly beneath him. He moaned something but Phil couldn't make it out; just two or three words said in a choking, bitter gasp of sound as he died looking straight up at the azure sky.

Phil kept watching the winner of that fight. You never could predict what a mankiller might do if something distracted him while he still had a gun in his hand. Sweat ran into Barker's eyes; it annoyed him and stung with salt, but he ignored it as the dark-visaged man stepped off Leffler's side of the road and slow-paced his way across, still holding his gun with the hammer back, and halted to scan the lifeless eyes of his victim. Satisfied, apparently, he put up the weapon, saw Phil, and said, 'It's all over, bartender. But next time I wouldn't rush out—I'd *look* out.' He turned to go back to his horse. He was untying the animal when Murph Crail came towards him with a cocked double-barrel shotgun in both hands.

'Hold it,' growled Murph. 'Keep your hands on the tie-pole, mister. Hey, Phil; walk in behind him an' lift out his gun.'

Barker was getting upright. He looked at Murph with strong disapproval, but in the end he did as he'd been asked; walked across and disarmed the dark-faced stranger, looked briefly at the gun, and was astonished to find the butt of the gun had the dead man's name on it. At least it had the same name on it: Dusty Froman.

'Walk,' growled Murph to the killer. 'Phil; come along, an' fetch his gun.'

Chapter Four

The killer sat in Murph's jailhouse-office answering questions easily and calmly. 'Sure I knew him, Sheriff. I knew him inside out. Why else would a man ride over a thousand miles to catch up with another man?'

Phil Barker was being discreet; after all, he was not the law, Murph was. Nevertheless Phil could think of a dozen better questions that Murph was now asking, so he leaned on the long front wall, listening and fidgeting, waiting for Murph to get on with it; get to the point and find out what had been behind it.

But Murph was in no hurry. He had the scattergun lying across his desk, and his hat atop the scattergun. In his right hand he was holding the pistol with the name 'Dusty Froman' across the back-strap. He held the gun up for his prisoner to see.

'Your name?' he asked.

The prisoner shook his head. 'No. That's my gun but that isn't my name. Dusty Froman was the man who died out there. Lemuel Froman, really, but folks been callin' him Dusty since he was knee high to a grasshopper.'

'An' have you known him that long?'

'Yup. Since we were both spindle-shanked kids.'

'Where was that, mister?'

'Montana. Lodgepole, Montana.'

Murph was impressed. 'That'd be one hell of a distance from here, wouldn't it?'

The killer nodded his head, putting a hard smile on his face. 'A hell of a distance. But the hardest part of all was coming through the mountains yonder.'

'How did you come by Froman's gun?'

'I picked it off the floor of a cabin lyin' beside a dead man.' The killer pointed. 'That ivory-butted gun Froman was carrying belonged to me. Look on the inside butt-strap. Those initials stand for Morgan Forrest.'

Murph looked, then handed the gun to Phil Barker who also examined it. Phil put the weapon gently down upon Murph's desk. He was about to burst with his desire to ask one question: Why?

Murph kept skirting all around it; he asked such inane questions as how the stranger had reached Douglas City, where he'd camped the previous night, and finally, if he'd ridden up to Froman's camp in the Bald Hills after leaving town about sun-up.

The lanky man said he'd been informed last night by the liveryman where Froman had his camp, and he had, as a matter of fact, ridden out there to kill Froman. He also said that was how he'd wanted to do it; with no witnesses, with no posse riding hard to catch him afterwards; with nobody upset nor involved, so that he could afterwards head straight back into the mountains and undertake his two-thousand-mile return trip.

'But he wasn't there; he struck camp, so I had to come back to your city—trailing him. You know the rest of it.'

'Not quite,' drawled big Murph Crail. 'Mister Forrest mind telling us *why* you killed Froman?'

Phil's agony eased off; he watched Morgan Forrest intently, anticipating some kind of logical answer.

Morgan's dark features were regular, hard and strong. He looked to be in his late twenties or early thirties. He had a direct gaze, an honest, candid way of speaking, and showed the kind of quiet, unwavering resolution a man would have to possess to do what he'd done—not just face down a man who'd obviously been plenty practised with guns, but to have also found his way through those mountains.

31

'I told you I found his gun beside a dead man in a cabin, Sheriff,' he stated. 'Well; that dead man was my cousin. We'd taken a year off from rangerindin' to hunt gold in the Bitterroot country. We didn't find much; two thousand dollars worth. Then Dusty came while I was out prospecting, killed my cousin, took the gold bag and headed out.'

'And left his gun,' blurted out Phil Barker, 'which would lead you to him?'

Forrest put a mild look upon Phil. 'Lead me to him? Mister; you've never made that ride or you wouldn't say a thing like that. I've been a year and a half on the trail. I lost it several times. Then I reached the far side of those mountains. Over in the valley folks told me no man in his right senses ever tried getting through the Coast Range. But they also told me the man with the ivory-stocked gun had headed into those mountains, so on I came. As for the gun—Dusty did that on purpose. He wanted me to know who'd killed Sam. He wanted to make me eat his dust, then he aimed to lose me and have his private laugh about that'

'You two were enemies?' asked Murph.

'Not especially, Sheriff. I just never had much use for Dusty. He wasn't much of a man in my opinion. I wasn't the only one felt that way. You can verify this by telegraphing to folks up at Lodgepole. He'd been picked up a couple of times; once for suspected cattle rustlling, again for a suspected murder—only no one ever found the body. He beat those arrests, and he might have beat Sam's murder too, by leaving my gun with the body. Only I didn't tell anyone what happened; that would've delayed me while there was an inquest and maybe a trial. Maybe even a prison stretch, or worse, for me, because I couldn't have proven I hadn't killed my cousin. Dusty figured that too.'

'Why wasn't there an inquest?' Murph asked.

'For the best reason under the sun, Sheriff. Because no one knew Sam was dead. Our cabin was in a pretty wild stretch of the Bitterroots. I simply buried him, turned his horse loose, took that gun on your desk—which I'd given to Dusty on his seventeenth birthday when we were still friends—and lit out. By now, of course, they may have found the grave; may even figure I killed Sam, but they may also figure we just pulled stakes and left the country.'

Murph looked up at Phil. The older man was studying Morgan Forrest with thoughtful eyes. He obviously was finding it hard to equate what he'd seen with what he'd just heard. Murph said, 'What d'you think?' to the saloonman.

Phil let his breath all out and offered no firm answer. 'I saw it head-on,' he stated. 'I can tell you they both went for their guns at the same time. Whatever happened up in Montana, Murph—this time it wasn't murder. Froman got off two shots. But there's something else . . .'

'Yeah; speak out, Phil. I either got a murderer here, or a man justified in what he done. An' I don't like riddles.'

'Mister,' Phil asked, looking straight at the killer. 'Why did you fire that third shot; he was down on his knees. He was finished. You could see that even from across the road.'

Morgan Forrest's eyes didn't even blink as he replied. 'Eighteen months riding like I've been doing, going hungry, going thirsty, getting lost in the Sierras, ducking bushwhackers, hostile bucks, make a man bitter, mister. Lying under the stars every damned night thinking of my cousin with that bullethole in his back—turns a man into more than just a manhunter. I gave him that bullet for my cousin, and I also gave it to him for what he'd done to me.'

Phil had no more to say. He too was a man who knew

33

B

what hatred could to to a person; he'd seen it warp and twist and completely alter other men. In his own past he could think back to matters he preferred to forget. He said, 'Well, Murph; I said it was a fair fight. This one called out to the other one first, an' like I told you before, they went at it hammer and tongs. Mister Forrest didn't murder Froman. I'll swear to that at the inquest. Only . . .'

'Yeah?' Murph said. 'Only what, Phil?'

'What're you goin' to do with him? He says send a telegram to Montana. We got no telegraph in Douglas City. If you lock him up it may take a month or better to get a letter sent up there, and an answer sent back.'

Murph had evidently already pondered that for he said, 'Lock him up and hold him. That's all I can do. I'm sure not goin' to set him loose an' have him disappear— then find out next month I set free an outlaw of some kind.'

Phil straightened up off the wall, he'd had his say, had heard the explanations, and beyond that the decisions weren't up to him. 'I got to get back to the saloon,' he said, and reached for the door.

For the time being that ended the matter; Murphy Crail locked Morgan Forrest in a cell and went forth to answer the questions of an astonished citizenry. Nothing like this had occurred in Douglas City before. There'd been gunfights and feuds, even some murders, but never so bizarre an affair as two men riding the length of the country, one fleeing, the other hunting, ending up out there in the morning-lighted roadway shooting it out with guns that didn't even belong to them.

Annie Standish had something to say the ensuing Sunday before church took up. Paul, her husband, was pre-occupied. When someone would elicit his opinion, Paul would shake his head in the best disapproving manner, but he didn't say much one way or another. He

34

The Bald Hills

was, however, a rare exception; the countryside, the ranges, the town, was engrossed, and meanwhile Cap Bozeman met with Phil Barker up at the saloon that same Sunday, to discuss an angle which Cap seemed to consider more pertinent than either the killing or the incarceration.

'All those jackals out there,' growled Cap, 'are making a Roman circus out of it. Froman's dead, Phil. That's what makes the difference, and the hell of it is, we didn't even know the man.'

'What's knowing him got to do with it?' Barker wanted to know.

'Use your head,' said Cap, unkindly. 'Froman's put us into a hell of a pickle. Oh; I know he refused to head up the cattle drive, but at least as long as he was alive there was a chance. Dead; the darned fool puts us deeper into hock to one another, plus eliminating any chance at all of us getting the drive headed up. Except for one thing.'

Phil nodded. 'Except for one thing. All right, Cap; what one thing?'

'Morgan Forrest.'

Phil carefully filled two glasses with his home-brew, skived off the foam and gravely placed one glass directly in front of Bozeman, just as gravely took the second glass for himself. He understood what Cap was driving at, finally. 'I don't think Murph would do it. In fact I know he wouldn't.'

'Pshaw,' snorted Cap Bozeman. 'He's got to do it. In the first place how's Murphy going to get his pay if the rest of us who make up the kitty don't have any money to put into it? In the second place, Murph's morally obligated to see that this community stays alive, which it damned well isn't going to be able to do pretty quick. In the third place—'

'Cap,' interrupted Barker quietly. 'Murph won't do it.'

35

'Phil Barker; he's *got* to do it. You listen here: Murphy can't hold Forrest. There was no murder committed, was there; nor any other actual crime. Then will you explain to me just how he can hold that man in jail?'

Barker thought that over and carefully began to look hopeful. He drank beer, wiped off the suds, and looked Bozeman straight in the eye. 'That's a right interestin' point o' view,' he said. 'Right interestin', Cap. How *can* Murph hold a man in his jailhouse who's committed no crime—unless of course he'd say defending himself against Froman was a crime.'

'Pshaw; how could that be? Self-defence's never been a crime. Now Phil; Mister Forrest also knows how to get back through the mountains. When Murph sets him loose—'

'Wait a minute, Cap. Suppose we went down an' had a talk with Mister Forrest. Suppose we sort of committed ourselves to help him, providing he'd do the same for us?'

Cap smiled broadly. Phil smiled right back. They lifted their beer glasses, touched them in silent salute, then drank.

Two rangeriders walked in out of the pleasant morning, hair slicked down, boots greased, most of the dust punched out of their reshaped hats. Phil groaned under his breath. They were the men who worked cattle on shares with Barker out on the saloonman's deeded acres.

Phil drew two more beers, skimmed them flat and set each glass before a cowboy. Those two were young, rawboned, spare men, pleasant-faced and tough-lipped. One of them eased his glass away, leaned down on the bar and said, 'Phil; we was just over to Leffler's store. He's in there nailin' boards over a busted window sore as hornet about that gunfight where the feller got killed out in the roadway. We asked him for another case of beans an' he said he wasn't goin' to be able to go on carryin' us much longer. Now, Phil; we kept our end o' the bargain; we minded the critters an' worked them, an' got 'em all ready to go.'

Barker held up a hand. 'A few more days,' he said. 'Cap and I were just discussing trailing them out through the mountains.'

The solemn pair of cowboys saw Cap down the bar. One of them said, 'How you figure to do that? Why not get some ships up here?'

'If we could get ships we'd have done it long ago,' Phil explained. 'If we wait much longer we'll be bankrupt. There's a feller in town who came through the mountains and—'

'Hell,' growled one rider in disgust. 'Phil; where you been lately? That feller got killed in a gunfight right out front of this here bar-room.'

'No. Not *that* one. There's another one. The man who killed *that* one. His name's Morgan Forrest.'

The second cowboy screwed up his face. 'Where is he now, Phil?'

'Well; Murph's got him locked up. But that's what Cap and I were talking about. Getting him out.'

The cowboys looked stonily at Barker. Phil reddened under those stares. He waved his arms. He said it wasn't nearly as impossible as it sounded; that he and Cap Bozeman were working up a plan. The cowboys, far from convinced, told Barker flatly that unless something were done within the next couple of days—week at the most—they were going to head down the coast and work for real wages, then come back for their share of the cattle-money when Phil finally, eventually, received it. Then they walked out of the saloon leaving Phil upset, angry, and thoroughly indignant.

Cap smiled his thin, wise smile. 'That's your part of it,'

he said. 'You got to go along. I'm already committed to goin' along. You know who that leaves?'

'Yeah,' mumbled Barker. 'Paul Standish. Come on; I'll lock the front door. We'll go catch him as he comes out of church and have a talk.'

Phil tossed down his apron, looking mean, dug for his keys and marched out into the empty, Sunday-morning roadway, locked his saloon and led the way southward, down towards the lower end of town.

Chapter Five

Annie Standish was annoyed when those two men, Bozeman and Barker, waylaid her husband outside the church and took him out of earshot with them. The congregation otherwise, though, ignored the seriously talking trio and carried Annie Standish along with it back up towards home.

Paul wasn't as difficult as Cap Bozeman and Phil Barker acted as though they'd thought he might be. He said, 'We've got to do something; I'm running short of money it's getting downright painful.' He agreed to go talk with Murphy, but he said he was just as dubious of success as Phil Barker had been.

Cap Bozeman never ruffled, always serene and half-amused, led the way. Murphy was feeding his prisoner when they entered. He couldn't help but notice the string tie and clean shirt on Standish, and the less presentable, workaday attire of the other two. He came out into his office and let them have their say, then he sat down and began shaking his head. Murphy Crail could be dogged when he wished to be. In fact, as Cap afterwards observed, Murph was as stubborn as a rock.

'I wrote a letter to the authorities up at Lodgepole, Montana,' he told them. 'A feller headin' south took it to be posted. Now, providing he don't forget to mail it, or don't lose it, I expect I should get back an answer in maybe three weeks. Dependin', of course, on someone comin' up this way, fetching it along. Meanwhile—'

'Murph,' exclaimed Phil Barker intently. 'Meanwhile, I'm going to lose my rangeriders, my cattle will stray into the mountains, and I'll be ruined.'

'You'll still have the saloon,' stated Murph, imperturbably.

Cap Bozeman tried next. 'Murphy; we'll send six good men with Mister Forrest. They'll have orders to watch him like a hawk, and to fetch him back when they return after selling the cattle. We'll have a clear-cut understanding with Forrest, as well.'

Murph shook his head. 'Six men or sixty, if he wanted to slip off in the night they couldn't stop him. If he did that half way through the mountains, what'd happen to your cattle then?'

'It's easy to see you've been a logger not a cowman,' stated Cap. 'The critters would turn about and backtrack themselves to grass again. We'd lose a few but—'

'Cap,' Murphy said, looking straight at the older man. 'I'm not going to set him loose. That's final.'

Cap's even temper began to fade slightly. He shot his answer right back. 'You can't hold him, Murphy. He's committed no crime. Right here stands your only eyewitness, and he says it was a clear case of self-defence. You've got no right to hold Mister Forrest.'

Murphy got a little angry too. He stood up, towering over the other three. 'I'm holding him, Cap. He's locked in an' he's goin' to stay locked in.'

Paul Standish, silent up to now, said, 'Can we talk to him? After all; he's the only one around who could tell us how to get through the mountains, and we've simply got to try it, Murphy.'

Sheriff Crail had no objection to this. He even escorted them into his cell-room and retrieved the dishes from Forrest's cell and departed with them.

The prisoner was a calm, almost stoic man. Without much doubt his travails of the past year and a half had marked him definitely for the rest of his life. He listened to Cap with quiet attention, and seemed to be studying all three of them at the same time. When Cap had finished he asked one question: 'What can you do for me? You say you'll work to get me out of here. Fine. But how? I heard Crail just now when he got mad out in the office. He isn't going to change his mind. I've already guessed that much about him.'

Paul Standish said, 'Mister Forrest; we've *got* to get you out of here.'

The prisoner didn't smile but his eyes brightened with slaty irony. 'And if I turn you down. . . ?' he said.

Phil Barker groaned a curse. This wasn't going at all as he'd anticipated. He'd been so positive Forrest would jump at the offer of help he hadn't once considered the possibility of a refusal. 'Listen,' he snapped. 'You'll rot in here, Forrest. That letter from Montana might never even reach Douglas City. The letter Sheriff Crail wrote about you may never even get mailed. All we want is your help getting our cattle through the mountains in exchange for your freedom. It strikes me we're not asking a whole lot.'

Morgan's grey eyes put that same ironic look upon Barker. 'I'll tell you this much, mister; a herd could be taken through the mountains. That's my business—cattle drives. But if you figure to bust me out of here—no thanks. I'd be running from the law as a fugitive for the rest of my life. I'd rather just wait this out. I'll be set free because you, as the only witness, know it was a fair fight.'

'But what about us?' asked Paul Standish.

Morgan Forrest leaned on the steel straps of his cell gazing outward. 'Get me out legally and I'll head up your drive through the mountains. But I want Sheriff Crail himself to open this door—not any one of you.'

Cap stood and tugged gently on his droopy moustache. He was eyeing Morgan Forrest with a shrewd, thoughtful look. He led the others back outside into the empty office, and yonder into the mid-day sunlight of the quiet

41

Sunday. He led them all the way back up to Phil Barker's saloon and said nothing until he had a glass of beer in his right hand. Then he got to the point very quickly.

'A circuit rider is down at Mattole holding court, which is sixty miles from here. I know, because I talked to the stagedriver night before last. We've got to get him to Douglas City then we've got to have Murph arraign his prisoner. If we work things right we should be able to do these things within the next three days. Paul; you ride to Matthole and fetch that judge up here. No; on second thought I'll do that. Paul; you'n Phil tell Forrest what we're doing, but you let me get a good head start before you also tell Murph.'

'Why?' asked Standish, puzzled. 'Murphy won't try to stop you.'

Cap was sly. 'Maybe not, but all I know is that right now Murph's across the fence from us, and we don't want to run into any more snags than we've already run into.'

They drank their beer, discussed their problem further a while longer, then Cap departed and Phil Barker offered Paul another beer, which was refused, then drew himself a second glass. 'This better work out,' he muttered dourly.

'It's *got* to work,' said Standish, and on second thought pushed out his glass for that refill. 'I had to dig into the sugar bowl for coins to put in the offering plate this morning It's *got* to work, Phil.'

Abe Sherman came ambling in for a beer. He said he'd just seen an odd thing; Cap Bozeman down at the liverybarn getting his top-buggy rigged out and putting a blanket-roll and a greasy sack of old jerky in the vehicle. Abe was mildly interested. 'What in the devil do you expect he's up to, goin' on a trip like that?'

'Go ask him,' growled Barker, in no mood for light talk.

42

The blacksmith considered those two unhappy countenances, then reached for his beer. 'Saw something else interestin' this morning too,' he murmured, drank deeply, wiped foam off his close-cropped whiskers and set the glass back down. The other two weren't paying any attention to him. 'Saw two strangers down at the liverybarn while Cap was gettin' rigged out, lookin' over that Froman feller's horse in the back corral.'

Barker's greyish, smoky gaze drifted around and settled upon Abe's face. Paul Standish also turned his head to regard the blacksmith. 'What kind of strangers?' asked Phil.

'Rangemen. Looked like they'd come overland. Appears to me there's gettin' to be a right smart trail worn through the mountains lately. First that Froman feller, then this Forrest feller, and now these two.'

Phil looked down at Abe's beer glass. 'Finish it,' he said sharply. 'I'm lockin' up for a while.'

He and Standish went outside, accompanied by Abe Sherman. Barker locked his roadside door for the second time, pocketed the key and struck out for the liverybarn. Paul and Abe went along with him. Standish was resolute and grim-faced. The blacksmith appeared to merely be interested. After all, aside from the fact that Douglas City was dead on Sundays, the appearance of two more strangers in town was a matter of interest.

But they were gone. The dayman said they'd asked about Dusty Froman, and after being informed he'd been shot to death, had then looked at Froman's horse, and after that, had gone over Froman's saddle as though they were thinking of buying it.

Phil wanted to know what else they'd said, if anything. The hostler knew very little more. 'They come in together, asked about Froman, then had me bait their horses with grain, looked around, asked about the

43

shooting scrape, got back astride and lit out towards the Bald Hills.'

'Wait a minute,' said Phil. 'Did you tell them where Froman's camp was?'

'Sure; they asked didn't they?' said the hostler.

Phil let that slide. He said next, 'What did you tell them about Morgan Forrest?'

'Well; they asked who'd killed Froman. I told 'em it was this Morgan Forrest feller, an' that Murphy Crail had him locked into a jailhouse cell. They asked if there was soon to be a trial and I said I sure didn't see how, since we got no judge in Douglas. An' that's about the size of it. Their horses had finished the grain, so they tugged up and rid off for the Bald Hills.'

Phil returned to the roadway and stopped. Abe was still tagging along but the saloonman ignored him. 'Paul; I'm gettin' a bad feeling,' he told Standish. 'Why would these strangers want to go look at Froman's camp?'

Standish didn't know. 'Maybe they're old friends,' he offered.

Phil scotched that with an oath that made Standish wince—after all, this was still the Sabbath. 'Old Friends want to visit the grave, not some old abandoned camp. Unless . . .' Phil dropped his voice so low Abe Sherman had to step in closer to hear his next words. 'Unless . . . they knew about that poke of gold Froman stole up in Montana, and are after it.'

Paul pondered a moment, looking surprised and perplexed. 'Two thousand dollars wouldn't have lasted him this long, Phil. Forrest said the killing up in Montana took place a year and a half ago.'

'Sure,' agreed Barker. 'Only somewhere on his backtrail Froman met these two; they saw his gold maybe, or he treated them to drinks and paid with raw gold. And they wouldn't know whether he only had two thousand dollars worth of the stuff or twenty thousand dollars worth. Tell me something; if a man was camped out in the Bald Hills all by hisself, and had gold on him, where'd he put it?'

'Bury it,' said Abe, not understanding what all this was about, but picking up the salient factors fast. 'Sure enough. He'd bury it in the ground, and that's what them two strangers are goin' out there to look for.'

Paul Standish was shocked. He looked up and down the empty, lethargic roadway with its soft-gold colouring and its quiet buildings. He looked back at Phil and turned to glance up towards the jailhouse. 'We better go tell Murph,' he finally blurted out, and would have started away but Barker caught his arm with an iron grip and swore again, his face twisted into an expression of indignant exasperation.

'You cussed idiot; if we go tell Murph he'll go out there twice as big as life and scare those men off.' Phil released his hold. 'Use your head, Paul. Froman turned us down on trailin' the cattle through the mountains. Forrest put enough stipulations on doin' the same thing that it amounted to the same kind of a refusal. But now there are two more strangers come into the Bald Hills country through the same blessed mountains ... You get my idea?'

Standish got it. He even improved on it. 'We don't tell Murph; we get our horses and go out there ourselves, and if those two strangers are after gold, we make them the same proposition about heading up the drive for us.'

Phil said, 'Go get your horse. Meet me over in front of the saloon in fifteen minutes. And for gosh sakes, put on another shirt without no tie.'

Standish walked away with a fresh spring to his stride. Phil watched him briefly, gave his head a hard little irritated wag, then started for the saloon, quite forgetting Abe Sherman, who tagged along, and who finally said,

'Phil; you're overlookin' something. Now I don't profess to understand all that's goin' on, but I do know one thing: You go slipping up on a pair of armed strangers who just might be a heap more than simply strangers—and you're darn likely to get salivated.'

They were across the road approaching the saloon when Barker snapped back at the blacksmith. 'I don't figure to slip up on 'em. We'll ride up out in plain sight and make our proposition.' He then halted in front of his building, dug out the door-key and fumbled briefly with it before turning around and saying, 'And who invited your furry nose to get stuck into our affairs anyway, Abe?'

Sherman retreated a step. 'No one. Nothin' to get mad about anyway. I just thought I'd make that suggestion.'

'Well; go make suggestions somewhere else, will you, Abe? I'm in trouble over those lousy cattle up to my ears.'

Sherman stood outside gazing after the thick, heavy torso of the barman as Barker stamped inside, on through and into the lean-to out back where he lived, to change his clothes and get ready to ride.

Then Sherman turned about and stood lost in thought for a while, eyeing the somnolent roadway. He was concerned; not because he was merely curious but also because he smelled trouble coming and didn't like the idea of seeing friends shot up.

He finally stepped out into the roadway, crossed over and started for the jailhouse. But when he got there Murphy was gone; he then went up to the restaurant, figuring Murphy was eating his noon meal, which proved to be correct, but by the time he'd related all he knew, Phil Barker and Paul Standish were already heading out of town in the direction of the Bald Hills, at a lope.

Chapter Six

It had never actually been any secret where Froman'd had his camp, for although he hadn't encouraged visitors and most of the rangeriders avoided him, they'd all spotted his camp a time or two, and had of course passed along this piece of information.

Phil Barker's two riders particularly had pinpointed that location for the saloonman because Froman had set up his camp within the generally accepted confines of Barker's deeded range.

Nevertheless, Phil took his time, once he cleared the forests and passed over into the hills themselves. He had Abe Sherman's warning in the back of his mind; he knew for a fact that men like these two could be deadly even when they had advance warning someone was approaching.

Paul, who also knew the Bald Hills well, said nothing. He appeared to understand what Phil was doing. And he had changed his shirt and had left that silly-looking shoestring necktie at home.

The Bald Hills were like giant anthills, not particularly tall nor pointed, but rather rounded and rolling, one after another. They'd perhaps been formed in prehistoric times on the bottom of the sea, but in any event they were loam all the way down. Rich loam at that, with scarcely any gravel or stone. They covered more miles than a man could ride over in quite a spell, and were green with lush grass at least ten months out of the year, and often they remained green even through the normal frosty periods as well. There were few places on earth so ideally perfect for cattle; for any and all ruminants for that matter, including the shy Coast Elk who at one time had roamed them exclusively, but which now had diminished to the point of extinction.

There was ample water. In fact, throughout Humboldt County water, at least a scarcity of it, had never really been much of a problem. Just the opposite was sometimes true; deluges sometimes came, in winter time, that threatened to wash the whole Pacific slope into the sea.

But in the spring the Bald Hills were as close to paradise as most stockmen ever thought they'd get, and in fact were as close to paradise as most of them wished to get. For Phil and Paul, who saw cattle by the hundreds, greasy-fat and blooming with the rich sheen found only in places where the grass had unexcelled nutrition, the sight lifted their spirits a little.

As Standish dourly observed, 'It's sure a mighty fine sight, seein' a man's critters topping out like this. Except that they are up here and they should be down in the San Joaquin country.'

Phil skirted around as long as he could, keeping their backs to the trees, but eventually he had to ride straight into the hills, and from there on they could be detected by anyone interested enough to sit his saddle atop a knoll watching for horsemen.

He still rode cautiously though. When they were within two and a half miles of their destination he went atop a hillock and halted to look across the mounded tops around them towards the place Froman'd had his camp.

'Too far,' he grunted, and rode down the far side seeking another vantage point closer in.

In this manner they covered another mile and a half. Then they headed for a somewhat higher knob in the middle distance, which cut their lead down still more. From this spot, Paul pointed. 'Two saddlehorses dragging their reins. You see 'em?'

Phil saw them. 'Where are the men?' he asked, and almost on cue, a carbine coughed from around some onward slope. Its bullet sang horse-high and two feet west of Paul. He started and swung off in one rapid movement. Phil did the same, but Barker also let off a surprised curse. The carbine was joined by another one, as invisible as the first one, but more accurate. Barker's horse dropped without a sound, struck squarely in the whorl between its eyes. If Phil had been astride and the horse hadn't had his head raised, that slug would have drilled him through the stomach.

Paul had only a sixgun. Phil had a booted carbine but he might as well have left it back in Douglas; the dead horse was lying flat upon the saddleboot with the gun inside it. Phil tugged and grunted to no avail.

For several long moments those invisible snipers were quiet. Paul, lying behind the dead horse, raised up to see, and one of the gunmen fired at him. He dropped flat, grim in the face and angry. That same bullet caused Barker to let go the carbine-stock and also flatten behind his dead mount. He was perspiring and red in the face, more from indignation than from his exertions.

'Where *are* they?' he hissed.

Standish, easing up on one side, peered around the round rump of the horse without his hat to make a long, slow study of the open, grassy land all around. He was pulling back to say something when that sharpshooter drove a slug to within four inches of where his head had been. Phil saw that and squirmed around to face the opposite end of his horse.

'One of them had slunk around the base of the hill below us on the right,' he exclaimed. 'And he's the marksman. We got to get that one, Paul.'

Standish didn't argue; his lips moved forming swear words but not out loud. Tomorrow, he might use them, if he were still alive tomorrow, but today was still the Sabbath, and although it put a mighty strain, Paul Standish, the lay-preacher, restrained himself.

Phil was worried for the first time. One of those men was as deadly as any man alive with a Winchester. The other one was also dangerous, but he seemed to still be on ahead down in the tall grass somewhere, not posing any immediate peril.

Paul dug dirt from his face and eyes, wiggled around until he could see the right-hand lip of their hillock, and pushed out his pistol, cocked and poised. That marksman just below them would have to show himself to fire again. Paul had what seemed to him to be ample reason for shooting the man—which was a paradoxical thing; he wouldn't use profanity on the Sabbath but he'd kill a man. That required a very peculiar variety of rationalization, but right then neither he or Phil Barker seemed to think it peculiar at all.

The man northwards of them fired his third shot. The bullet was wide and slightly high. They didn't answer that man, but continued watching for the other one.

Then a long lull came. Evidently the prone man down there below the lip of their knoll in the grass knew they were waiting for him. He made no attempt to raise up again.

The heat wasn't bad but all the same they were suffering down there behind that dead horse. Discomfort was added to by thirst, and after they'd been pinned down like that for a long half hour, also by the infinitely more demoralizing uncertainty.

Phil was restless. He told Paul to stay where he was and give Barker cover. Then the saloonman began inching his way straight towards the sharpshooter through the tall grass. He hadn't progressed thirty feet when Paul hissed. Phil turned irritably. Paul pointed behind them, down across the same country they'd covered getting up where they now were.

'Two riders coming,' said Paul in a stage-whisper. 'And coming fast. One of them is big enough to be Murphy Crail. I'm sure that's his big grey horse.'

Phil began slithering backwards to get into the shelter of his dead horse again. While he did this Paul kept an intent watch over where their grassy little hill sharply dipped and went out of sight, down where that marksman was hiding.

Barker risked raising his head for a second or two, then dropped down. The gunman northward and around the slope of his hill, cut loose. He always seemed to fire to the right, as though his sights had been damaged somehow, and the man didn't realize it so he could compensate for the drift.

That gunshot carried well. Phil and Paul saw those two riders yank back and slow to a fast walk as they came on. The unseen marksman under their hill had evidently also sighted the oncoming men because they heard rapid, frantic scufflings down there as though that gunman was trying to get away fast.

Paul started forward as though to try a shot at the man, but Phil hauled him back. Those riders were splitting up now, one taking the left side of their hill, the other one heading around the right side. They were close enough now to be recognized. One was Abe Sherman, the other one was Murphy Crail, and both had their carbines out and ready.

Phil, following the progress of bearded Abe Sherman, said, 'Hell; that idiot Abe is goin' to ride right over the top o' that sharpshooter.' He jumped up into a low crouch and hurled himself ahead. At once the man who always shot to the right, let fly. He missed as usual, but it was close enough to make Phil drop flat. He was close enough to the edge of the slope anyway. He poked his sixgun out, aimed at something below and to his left, then fired.

Paul heard him curse. He cocked and fired again. That time he cocked the single-action .45 but tilted it up in his fist, intently watching something out of Paul's vision. Finally, he cast a look over his shoulder and said, 'Got him, Paul. Got him as he was scuttlin' between our hill and back where his friend lies.'

Suddenly two carbines opened up fast, the explosions seeming to blend in a furious duel on the left side of the hill. Paul crawled rapidly over to see. He called back to Phil Barker.

'Come see this; Murphy's got the other one on the run back towards those loose horses.'

Murph was firing one-handed. It was not just inaccurate, it was also haphazard since his big grey was buck-running like a frightened jack-rabbit. But the man on foot up ahead of Murphy Crail was running even harder, and when he whirled to squeeze a shot now and then, his aim was even worse. In the end, this man, having fewer slugs in his carbine, hurled the thing away when it went dry, and went for his handgun. That was a mistake; if he'd kept running at least he'd have been helping himself, but the moment he swung to stand wide-legged and aim, Murphy dropped off his horse, swung the beast and lay the Winchester atop the seating-leather. 'Drop it,' he bawled in vibrant anger, 'Or I'll kill you!'

The man stood awkwardly crouched into a stiff posture, gun half drawn, staring into the solitary eye-socket of Crail's carbine. He very slowly finished his draw and dropped the gun into matted grass at his feet.

Phil stood up, he and Paul went hastening down the opposite side of their knoll where Abe Sherman's

52

garrulous voice came up to them ardently scolding some-one down there.

When they reached Abe he looked around at them and said caustically, 'I told you so. Phil Barker, I warned you against somethin' like this. By all rights Murph an' I shouldn't have come. We should've left you to stew in your own juice. By rights we should've.'

Barker swept Abe with one glance, stepped ahead and stopped where he had the wounded man in his view. From atop that knoll he'd tried to aim at the gunman's broad back. He'd broken the man's leg just above the ankle.

Paul also stepped in close and dispassionately eyed the grimacing, writhing marksman. 'Good shouting,' he said gravely, and Phil had his answer ready.

'Aimed low. Figured we should take 'em alive if we could.'

They knelt to tie off the spurting blood. The marks-man scarcely heeded their hostile presence at all. He was patently in great agony.

They tied off the bleeding, disarmed the sharpshooter, and looked up from this messy chore only when big Murph Crail came riding around the shoulder of their hill herding a crestfallen, sweaty and badly upset captive ahead of him. At the sight of those three on their knees in the grass, blood-splattered, and his companion lying there panting in agony, the prisoner stopped and gasped.

Murph alighted. He was in a bad mood. He yanked the injured man to his feet and held him one-handed as though he'd been a doll. 'How come you to be ridin' around my county takin' shots at folks?'

'Doctor,' gasped the anguished man, 'Get me to a medic, Sheriff, before all the blood leaks out'n me.'

Murph fiercely shook the man, thrusting his angry face

53

in close. 'I asked you a question, mister: Who the hell you think you are, ridin' into the Bald Hills country and shootin' at innocent folks?'

The gunman didn't answer. Nor did roiled-up Murphy Crail shake him again. The wounded man passed out and hung there until Murph put him back down in the grass and sent Abe for the horses. Then he turned on Barker and Standish with a sparking glare.

'Who do you think *you* are?' The surprised men stood gaping. '*I'm* sheriff in this county,' went on Murphy Crail. '*I'm* the one who investigates strangers. Suppose you'd gotten killed. You know what folks would have said? They'd have said that doggoned Murphy Crail's too lazy to stir his stumps and now look what's happened. That's what they'd have said. I ought to heave you two into jail too. If it hadn't been Abe come told me what you were up to, these fellers'd have finished you off atop that cussed little knoll.'

Murph paused because he ran out of breath, but his glare was just as sulphurous, still, when the horses arrived. Abe had stripped the rigging off the dead animal and had it tied behind his own saddle.

They put the injured man astride one horse, put his friend atop another horse, tied both their arms behind them, then Phil and Paul had to ride Paul's horse together, one in the saddle, one behind it. Murphy led off, his broad back rigid with righteous indignation. He had nothing more to say to Barker and Standish.

Abe did though; he wanted to know if anyone had gone over to Froman's old camp to see if the captives had dug up anything. Right then nothing was farther from the minds of all the others than thoughts of a hypothetical buried pouch of gold.

The injured man fainted twice before they reached town. They finally put his partner over close and set his arms free so he could support the other man. They were both rough-looking, unkempt, slab-hammed men; range-riders by their looks, but evidently they also had an occasional sideline. But all the fight was out of them by the time Douglas City was reached in the early evening.

Chapter Seven

Murphy Crail was impressive even to men who'd known him long enough to be accustomed to his size and heft, but to men such as those two strangers, Murphy must have seemed gigantic because he was mad. This mood didn't often assail Murphy Crail; he was ordinarily too phlegmatic; but when he did get angry, he got angry all over and he remained that way for a long time.

He and the other three men waited in the quiet background while the local liveryman, who was a rather good homoeopathic veterinarian, repaired the injured leg of the wounded prisoner.

A number of people had seen them arrive in town, and that started local gossip mills to grinding. As far as the men in Murph's jailhouse were concerned gossip was as remote and irrelevant as the moon. They gave the injured man a solid slug of rye whiskey from a bottle kept in a cupboard, and sat watching the man's colour return.

The liveryman left as soon as he'd finished. Their wounded man held out his hand for the bottle. Murph handed it over and reprovingly watched those two, the uninjured captive as well as the injured one, got to work half killing his bottle. When he got it back Abe Sherman also held out a hand. Murph handed the bottle over but he wasn't very gracious about it. Paul and Phil both had a respectable couple of swallows.

Murph crossed to the bench the wounded man was lying upon. Nearby in a chair sat his partner, silent as a rock, but watching everything that happened. Murph tapped the injured man on the chest.

'What's your name?' he asked.

'Dobe Hill.'

Murph looked at the man. 'Very funny. But I'm not laughin'.'

'Sheriff,' spoke up the other captive, 'that's the truth. His last name is Hill. Folks call him Adobe for a nickname. 'Dobe Hill.'

Murph studied the earnest face of the uninjured man and said, speaking in a less harsh tone. 'What's *your* name?'

'Stanley Foley.'

'Mister Foley; what the devil do you fellers mean ridin' around bushwhackin' folks?'

'We thought they was redskins after our horses.'

Phil Barker snorted derisively. 'Murph; he's lying. They could see we weren't redskins when they first shot at us.'

Foley was a heavier, craftier edition of his partner, but they were both about six feet in height, and marked with the scars of travel, hard living, and toughness. Foley regarded Phil Barker for a moment, venomously, then almost insolently swung his face back towards Murphy Crail.

'Sheriff: we were over near that abandoned camp and seen these two tryin' to sneak up on us. So we just decoyed 'em with our loose horses, and crawled up to meet 'em in the grass.'

Murphy tapped the wounded man again. 'What've you got to say?' he asked.

'Dobe Hill's light-blue eyes lifted to Murph's hostile features. 'You can got to hell. That's what I got to say.'

Murph wasn't in a very tolerant frame of mind. He caught hold of Hill's shoulder, hauled him up the bench and held him in a sitting position with that splinted, bandaged leg lightly touching the floor. Adobe Hill groaned and rolled hating eyes at Murphy Crail.

To Paul Standish and Phil Barker this was a clumsy scene. Phil was especially annoyed by it. He said, 'Cut it out, Murph. I'll tell you my guess about these two.' Phil proceeded to sketch his theory about the strangers and their purpose for being out at Froman's camp site.

Murph thoughtfully ingested all this and went over to sit in front of his desk studying the captives. He finally said, 'We got no judge in Douglas City. He doesn't show up but about once a year. Hill; you'll be walkin' as good as new by the time he gets here. Foley; you'll have a good long rest. I've got another prisoner too. Maybe you boys'll know one another.'

Foley said, 'The hell with your other prisoner. How can you cal'clate to hold us when all we done was protect ourselves against these two skulkers tryin' to get up close enough to bushwhack us?'

'It's easy,' replied Murph. 'I just toss the pair of you into a cell and forget you until the circuit rider gets up this way again.' Murph started to leave his chair.

Foley said, 'Wait a minute; how about those two?' He pointed an accusing finger at Barker and Standish.

Murph had an answer for that. 'One owns the local saloon. The other one lives in town, but he has a ranch in the Bald Hills. I didn't know they were up to something, this morning, until they were already in trouble. But whatever else they are, they aren't bushwhackers an' they weren't after your horses, nor your lives. You heard what the saloonman said—you two knew Froman and come here to get his poke of gold.'

'Why, dang it all,' broke in Stan Foley, straightening up with quick indignation. 'We'd hardly reached the camp. Anyway, Froman's dead. The dayman at your town liverybarn told us that. An' besides; we didn't even know Froman.'

'Another lie,' exclaimed Phil Barker. 'If you didn't know him how come you to look over his outfit down at the liverybarn, then high-tail it straight to his camp?'

'Curiosity,' growled Foley, staring daggers at Phil

58

Barker. 'Any law against bein' curious?'

Adobe Hill said, 'That's right. Anyway, we needed a place to camp and figured if this other feller'd had a decent spot, we'd take it over.'

Phil rolled up his eyes. Even Abe Sherman and Paul Standish showed unmistakable signs of disbelief. Murph studied his prisoners. 'How'd you get through the mountains?' he asked.

Foley's eyes jumped from Murph to his partner and back again. Evidently this question, out of context to their previous line of conversation, threw him for a loss. It sometimes happened even with the best of liars.

Hill said, 'We followed someone's trail.'

Barker said, 'I'll bet you did. Only you thought those tracks belonged to Froman and they belonged to Morgan Forrest.'

Both the captives looked quickly at Barker. 'Who is Morgan Forrest?' one of them muttered. 'Never heard of him.'

Phil threw up his hands. 'Murph; you got a prize package of professional liars here. They knew who Morgan Forrest was; the liveryman told them they asked who'd killed Froman.' Phil stood up. 'Come on, Paul; it's gettin' too deep in here for me.'

After those two left, only Abe Sherman and Murphy Crail remained with the prisoners. Abe hadn't said a thing; he stood by the door stroking his furry face. It was difficult to tell what he was thinking.

But it was no secret what Sheriff Crail was thinking. He said, 'Froman didn't have any gold.' Waited until the sceptical expressions dimmed a little upon the faces of his prisoners, then said, 'He stole a couple thousand dollars worth up in Montana, but that was eighteen months back, if the information I got is correct. Now you know eighteen hundred in gold or silver isn't enough to keep a man living good for almost two years.'

59

'Who told you it was only two thousand?' asked Adobe Hill. 'They sure roped you in, Sheriff.'

Murph smiled. 'So it *was* the gold you were after. Well; that's too bad because there isn't any.'

Foley suddenly turned towards Hill. 'I told you on the trail,' he said fiercely, 'if he stopped in some town they'd cut his throat an' plunder him the first time he laid down a gold coin for a drink.'

Murph's smile faded. 'Gold *coin*? It was raw gold.'

Foley shook his head with an accusing look upon his face. 'Cut it out, Sheriff,' he growled. '*You* got it. But you're goin' to have trouble keepin' it. I give you my word on that.'

Abe Sherman was baffled. Murph was slow grasping what was being implied here until he spoke once more, and got back one more answer.

'I suppose you figure you'll get a share of it,' he said.

Adobe Hill nodded his head up and down looking straight at Murphy Crail. 'Sheriff; any time a feller steals a ten thousand dollar shipment of gold coin off a Frisco-bound bullion coach and takes to the hills with it, he lives numbered days because it ain't just the two-bit punks wearin' tin badges who get on his trail. I'm tellin' you for a fact, what Stan just said is true; you're goin' to have one hell of a time keepin' that money.'

Abe felt weakly for a chair and collapsed into it. Murph sat and regarded his captives without moving or uttering a sound for a full two minutes. He only looked away from them once, and that was to glance at the closed roadside door as though he were wishing Standish and Barker were still in the office.

Finally, he got up, took his captives into the cell-room, locked them in without a word or glance at Morgan Forrest in the adjoining cell and marched back out again. He then took Abe Sherman in tow and headed for Phil Barker's saloon. When they were half way along he stopped, turned and looked down into the hairy face beside him. 'Abe; you keep your mouth closed. You understand me? You don't talk to no one at all about what we know.'

The blacksmith nodded. 'How about you?' he then said. 'What you going' to tell Phil and Paul Standish?'

'They'll have to know. But no one else.'

'Not even Cap Bozeman?'

Murph studied on that a spell. Cap was sort of unofficial *alcalde* of Douglas City. At least that's what they called them southward where Spaniards had, in the early days, set up all governing authority. An *alcalde* was something of a mayor, judicial dignitary and, in a pinch, father-confessor. Usually, he was someone esteemed in a community.

'Well. Maybe Cap'll have to be told too,' assented Murph. 'But that's all.'

'How about—?'

'Abe; I said that was all. Now you remember this. Don't you tell a soul.'

Sherman nodded again, and again offered mild dissent. 'Only I don't see what difference it'll make. Folks are goin' to find out soon enough.'

'I'll spell it out for you,' growled big Murphy Crail. 'We got a nice, peaceful town here. But if Froman had *twenty* thousand in gold coin he robbed off some coach after he got down into California, what Hill said was correct. There'll be bounty hunters, treasure hunters, lawmen, and probably free-lance murderers on his trail like buzzards after an ailin' cow. That means we'll get more strangers—with guns. It also means, if the local folk hear about the money, they'll go dig up Froman's camp site too, an' when those two sets of men meet, there's goin' to be a doggoned war, more'n likely. *Now* do you understand why you got to keep silent?'

'Yes,' stated the blacksmith. 'But I got one question, Murph.'

'You're full of 'em. Spit it out an' let's get on up to the saloon.'

'Murph; where *did* Froman hide that gold bullion?'

Sheriff Crail glowered for a moment, then caught the older smaller man by the arm, swung him around and started across the road in the direction of the bar-room with him as he said, 'Abe; I'm warnin' you. If you go up there pokin' around I'll slap you in the same cell with Foley and Hill. And you'd better believe it.'

There were about two dozen idlers in Phil Barker's saloon, mostly idling along the bar-front drinking beer or an occasional shot of whiskey. They looked up when Murph and Abe walked in, but otherwise showed no great amount of curiosity. They'd heard of course, from Phil and Paul, about the skirmish in the Bald Hills, but since neither Barker nor Standish knew *why* that fight had flared up, they couldn't tell much more about it.

Murph took a corner table in the shadows, jerked his head for Phil to come on over, and sent Abe to fetch Paul Standish who was at the opposite end of the bar, sipping a beer.

Murph didn't waste words. When the four of them were seated he jumped right in, brushed aside all interruptions until he was finished, then he leaned back looking at the astonished faces of Standish and Barker. In the back of Murph's mind was the solid knowledge that money, any kind of money, was desperately needed by these men. Not only by them, either. That was what worried him most. That, and the indisputable fact that *someone* sooner or later, was going to go into the hills and try to find Froman's cache. If the word leaked out, there'd be a regular gold-rush, a genuine stampede—and in all probability, also a head-on collision between the local men and whoever was coming through the hills, also on the trail of that stolen ten thousand in gold coin.

Paul was so startled by Murph's revelation he forgot it was still Sunday and said, 'I'll be damned.'

Phil, just as astonished, was more earthy in his unprintable exclamation. Then they all sat staring at one another.

Chapter Eight

But the hardest man to convince Froman'd had twenty thousand in gold, not just whatever might have remained of the two thousand he'd stolen up in Montana, was Morgan Forrest. He and Abe, Murph, Phil and Paul sat in the lamplighted sheriff's office after most of Douglas City had gone to bed, looking at one another.

It had been Phil's suggestion they bring Forrest out of his cell and tell him, because Forrest was the only one who might have heard about this stage hold-up; after all, he'd been on Froman's trail for eighteen months. And, as Phil had said up in his saloon, first off, they had to be certain those lying bushwhackers were telling a possible truth. Secondly, they had to know if Forrest thought Froman might really have cached that money somewhere in the Bald Hills.

Forrest's reaction was negative. 'I heard of a stage hold-up over in the San Joaquin Valley, down near a place named Benecia. But no one said Froman had done it. In fact, it happened the day after I rode into Benecia and no one seemed to know who'd done it or how much they got. I didn't stay in Benecia; all I wanted was to find out if Dusty Froman had been there and which way he'd ridden out. The liveryman told me and I pulled out that same night.'

'Those two men I locked into the cell next to you,' said Murph, 'told us that for a fact.'

Forrest was smoking a cigarette with his shoulders against the log wall. He looked ironic, almost amused, by the expressions of solemn gravity on the faces before him. 'How would Froman know such a bullion shipment was being made?' he asked.

'Luck,' suggested Phil. 'He hit a coach and got the jackpot. It happens every now and then.'

Forrest took a long drag and exhaled grey smoke. 'Ten thousand in gold coin?' He shook his head a little. 'I don't believe it. That kind of a coincidence only happens once in a blue moon.'

Murph was being stubborn. '*I* believe it,' he told the others.

Abe said mildly, 'Murph; they lied about other things.'

Murphy wouldn't be budged. 'Why would they lie about this?' he wanted to know. 'What good would it do them? None at all.'

Paul Standish offered the opinion that stopped their wrangling. 'There's sure one way to *know* whether they're lying or not,' he said, and would have said more but Murph broke in with a low growl.

'We can't find the gold and we got no way except through letters, of writin' down to Benecia to make certain, without havin' to wait a month for an answer.'

'Let me finish,' said Paul. 'What I was going to say was—we don't have to find Froman's cache and we don't have to take the word of Foley and Hill.'

'How then?' demanded Murphy.

'Wait,' replied Paul. 'Just wait. If it's true there'll be others come through the mountains looking for Froman *and* his loot. They'll tell the same story Hill and Foley told, Murph. That'll be enough proof for me.'

'And me,' agreed Morgan Forrest.

Phil and Abe nodded, watching the sheriff. Murphy wrestled with this suggestion a while then reluctantly agreed it made sense. Then he warned the others against speaking to anyone other than the men right at that moment in his office, about the gold cache or anything else which pertained to the bullion.

They all agreed, but Morgan Forrest said, 'Sheriff; I

65

want out of here. You've got no charge anyway.'

Murph turned back to this familiar topic with evident relief. 'I got a good enough reason to hold you, Forrest; we're waiting for a judge to come along.'

'All right,' stated Forrest. 'But meanwhile I'm entitled to freedom on bail.'

Murphy scowled fiercely at Forrest. 'If there's one thing I never liked,' he grumbled, 'it's book-learnt cowboys. You can't post no bail because I don't know how much it should be.'

Phil moved into the conversation at this point. 'Take his horse an' saddle; hold them, Murph.'

'You tend bar and I'll tend the law,' snapped Murph, arising, going over and opening the roadside door. 'Now you fellers remember; no talk to anyone at all. Not even to each other if someone else happens to be within listenin' distance. Now go on home. I'll see you in the morning.'

When Murphy closed the door and turned, Morgan was watching him from below the half-droop of lids. 'The biggest mistake,' he murmured, 'was to tell them at all.'

Murphy resumed his seat at the desk as he replied to that. 'I had to. The blacksmith was in the room when Foley and Hill shot off their mouths. Sherman's a good enough feller, in his way, but he'd have told Barker anyway. Not Standish, likely, because they aren't exactly close friends, but Sherman and Barker are. Anyway; I had no idea Foley and Hill were going to say anything like that, until it just came out. Then it was too late to keep it a secret.'

'Sheriff,' Morgan Forrest said, 'just how long do you think it'll be, before folks start slipping out of town with shovels and picks—and guns?'

Murph didn't answer right away. Like all lawmen, even ones in isolated communities like the Bald Hills country of far Northern California, he knew perfectly well that there was no such thing as a real secret. 'I don't know. But if it comes down to that, Forrest, it's not the folks tearin' up Froman's old camp searching for that cache that worries me. It's the trouble that'll pop sure as shootin' if the local folks tangle with a bunch of brush-poppers who've been on Froman's trail like Foley and Hill—and you—were.'

'There's a way out, Sheriff.'

Murph looked up quickly but doubtingly. 'How?'

'Go out there yourself, locate the cache, and beat everyone else to it. Haul it back here and lock it up until you can send it down to San Francisco to whoever it belongs to down there.'

'You sure get wild ideas,' growled Murph. 'How the devil could I find it?'

Forrest put out his smoke, swept up his hooded eyes and said, 'By yourself, Sheriff, you couldn't, because you didn't know Dusty Froman well enough to have any idea where he'd hide something. But with me along, your chances would be fair. At least they'd be better than they'd be any other way.'

'Oh no,' said Murphy, rolling his brows together. 'You don't talk yourself out of this jailhouse, mister. Not on your—'

'Sheriff; I'm not trying to talk myself out. Sure; I want out, but it's not so important to me as all that. Frankly, it's the boredom—the sitting in there staring at log walls—that's making me restless. You have my guns and if you like I'll ride out there with you with both wrists tied. But if you don't get that cache first—providin' one really exists—you're going to be inviting exactly what you're trying now to avoid—shooting trouble.'

Murphy got up, went over and rattled the grate in his little iron stove, shot a look back and said, 'You mean—tonight?'

'There's no better time, Sheriff. And there's no guarantee we'll find it. But by tomorrow it'll likely be too late to even try. And one more thing; if we *do* find it and leave the place looking like that gold has been secretly dug up and taken away, it's going to discourage not just your local treasure-hunters, but also whatever bounty-hunters and other riff-raff who're on their way to find it.'

Murph rattled the grate again, peered inside to see whether or not he'd shaken loose all the ashes, then fumbled in a wood-box for kindling to light the stove with. It was getting chilly.

After he had a small fire going, Murphy resumed his seat at the desk and moodily studied Morgan Forrest. He had a problem; he wanted to trust Forrest because soon now he was going to have to trust someone, and yet Forrest wasn't a man it was easy to be familiar with; at least not familiar enough to put a man's whole faith in.

Still; what Forrest had just said made sound sense. Providing of course, as he'd also said, there was a cache out there at Froman's camp site. Another factor favouring the idea was that it was now late, most folks were abed, and Murph could spirit his prisoner out of town without being observed. Finally; as Forrest had pointed out, tonight was the ideal time to make the search.

He looked at his broad hands, saying, 'You think you'd know where Froman might hide something?'

'I've known him most of my life. We were partners once, when we were in our teens. That's when I gave him that pistol with his name on the butt-strap. No, Sheriff, I wouldn't say I'll know right where to go to find that cache. Dusty Froman changed into something a lot different than what he was as a kid, these past eight or ten years. But I *did* know him well, and after being on his trail for the past year and a half, I learnt a lot about the kind of man he'd become. I think *maybe*, between the two of us, we *might* find the cache—if there really is one. I also think if we don't do it tonight, it's going to be too late tomorrow night.'

'Well damn it all,' exclaimed Murphy, standing up and stalking around his small office like a caged bear, 'All right, Mister Forrest.' He halted, turned and said, 'And I'll kill you the first wrong move you make. Is that understood?'

Morgan Forrest nodded, also standing up. Murph glowered a moment longer, then set his hat, went to the door and opened it to look out, turned back and told Forrest to turn down the lamp and come along.

Getting horses posed no problem although the night-man at the liverybarn, the same night-man who'd originally talked to Forrest when he'd arrived in Douglas, looked long and hard at Murphy Crail, saying nothing out loud but obviously keeping up a hell of a thinking.

They left town by riding on out the back of the barn and drifting on up northerly for a short ways, then cutting westerly through the star-splashed night. There was a moon but high gossamer clouds drifted across it almost continually. During the infrequent periods when it was allowed to show through, the land brightened to a ghostly phosphorescence. It took them a considerable length of time to get near the Bald Hills, but neither man was in a big hurry. Murphy Crail had a shovel stuck into the carbine-boot under his right leg and he'd also borrowed a crowbar from the night-man at the barn. These though were their only implements. Murphy wasn't optimistic; in fact he wasn't even anxious to get up there and see if they could locate Froman's cache. As he said, when they passed eventually over into the first low, grassy roll of the Bald Hills, 'I just can't figure Froman packin' up, rolling his bedroll and all to leave

69

the country, and leaving behind anything like ten thousand dollars in gold coin. It doesn't make sense to me.'

'Not even if he meant to come back for it, Sheriff?' asked Forrest. 'Not even if he had no way to carry that much solid weight on one horse?'

Murph was dogged about that. 'That'd have to be the only two sensible reasons,' he allowed, and fell to studying Forrest. He hadn't bothered tying his prisoner, as Forrest had suggested, so now they rode along side by side not visibly captor and captured, but more like friends on a late-night trail. Murph wanted to believe in Forrest. Aside from the lanky, swarthy man's confidence and unruffled calm, he seemed to be a man worth knowing. Still; Murphy was suspicious. Not just over the way he'd killed Dusty Froman, his former friend, but also because Forrest made no attempt to be friendly. He was a loner; that was obvious, but more than that, he seemed almost anti-social.

'Y'know,' Murphy said at last. 'If those folks up in Montana send me word they figure you killed your cousin up there, I'm goin' to have to send you back to them chained like a captive bear.'

Forrest smiled over at Murphy. 'If that happens, Sheriff, you'll have reason not to trust me. Up to now I've been concentrating on just one thing so long, now that it's over I'm having trouble picking up the pieces of my life the way it used to be. But I don't want to keep on with this, now that Froman's dead, so I'll tell you frankly—if they send for me to be tried up in Montana, you nor anyone else is ever going to get me there.'

Murphy nodded, not the least bit annoyed by his prisoner's candour. 'I'd do the same,' he admitted, and reined off to bypass the hills and keep to the lower, twisting little pathways at their bases. 'If they *don't* want you back, then I'll have to make it right with you for

70

keepin' you locked up.' Murphy was frank about this. 'If you'd stay in the country Phil'd maybe take you on workin' cattle with him on shares. The men he's got now have just about had enough since this trouble over shipping the herds came up. It's not a bad thing, either. You do all the work, he puts up the land and livestock, then the pair of you split down the middle when the critters are sold.'

'Doesn't sound bad at all,' murmured Morgan Forrest, but he was studying the onward hills in the glowing night, sounding uninterested in Phil Barker and his share-crop cattle operation. 'When I rode out here before, Sheriff, I skirted around more to the west and came to the camp from down out of the north-west. Gave me a better view all around, in case there was some reason for not riding on up.'

Murphy nodded and wordlessly followed this advice. It took them another hour but they had all the balance of the night anyway, and it made cautious good sense to-boot.

Forrest halted, finally, when they were side by side upon a lower hill above the creek which ran near Froman's old camp site. He and Murphy Crail sat like carved images saying nothing and very carefully study-ing the land all around. Murphy finally showed by point-ing where the wounded man and his friend had tried to ambush Phil Barker and Paul Standish.

Forrest listened courteously, but the moment Murphy ceased talking he said, 'Let's go; there's no one down there.'

They reached the camp without incident. Except for the limbs on a little tree and the flimsy pole-corral Froman had erected, the place was still and lonely and totally empty. That small watershed made a musical sound in the chilly night, not noticeable though until they were on the edge of the camp.

Around them they had an excellent sighting in all directions. Forrest dryly commented about this, saying 'After a while men like Froman got to be, sort of get the knack of thinkin' like wild animals. They never lie down at night without having all the escape-routes in their minds, and they never make a camp where they can't see someone coming before someone sees them. It'd be a hell of a way to live.'

They dismounted and put their animals into the little flimsy corral, walked over where the stone-ring lay with its nest of wood-ash, and hunkered there. Murphy said, 'All right, mister; sniff us up a track or a scent or somethin'.'

Forrest sat and looked and said nothing for a long while. 'When I was here before,' he murmured finally, 'I only spent a few minutes; just long enough to see he'd struck his camp. But it struck me then, that of all his cold camps I'd been in for the past year and a half, this one was the first he'd made that looked like he'd meant to stay a spell.'

'What's odd about that?' asked Murphy, gazing around.

'Dusty Froman never stayed in one place more than two nights, Sheriff. I'd say he was in this one nearly a month.'

'At least a month,' agreed the lawman. 'Maybe more; the first most of us knew he was in the country was when some of the rangemen saw his pole-corral and passed word around there was a stranger campin' out here. So it could've been even two months.'

'That is interesting,' murmured Forrest, and stood up from the fireplace to turn slowly from the waist, studying all the little trails, the dusty places where a man had bedded down, and the creekbank where he'd no doubt knelt to wash and dip water up. 'It's got to be close by then. Fetch the shovel and crowbar; let's go to lookin'.'

Murph wasn't very hopeful but he got the tools and ambled along behind his prisoner, privately thinking he should've had his head examined for ever undertaking this hare-brained scheme.

C*

Chapter Nine

No one could have been more thoroughly astonished than Murphy Crail when, after walking up and down the creekbank for some time, Morgan took the shovel, paced off several yards and began to dig where a little wilting patch of choke-berries grew, because the ground came up very easily, as though it had been disturbed before, and also because, after twenty minutes of hard work, Morgan Forrest stepped aside from the hole he'd dug and beckoned the sheriff on up. There it was in little doeskin bags. The shovel's tip had broken one and dull gold shone up to them in the misty moonlight.

'Lord Almighty,' gasped big Murph, and got awkwardly down into the hole to kneel and closely examine the cache. He wasn't conscious of having his back to his prisoner until he looked over his shoulder and saw that Forrest was holding the forty-five he'd easily lifted from Murph's holster as Crail had clambered down into the dug-hole. Forrest smiled at him. Murph stood up very slowly, turned and held out his hand. 'Give me that gun,' he growled. Forrest laid the weapon on Murph's extended palm, still smiling. Murph's neck was red. He passed over this small but significant incident by saying, 'I'll pass the little bags up to you.'

But Murph didn't recover from his shock even after they'd emptied the cache. 'How in hell did you know?' he asked.

Forrest pointed. 'The choke-cherries,' he said. 'They're wilting. This close to water it couldn't be drought causing it. There hasn't been any frost. And Froman was a clever

74

The Bald Hills

cuss in his own way. Given another few weeks the bushes would've firmed up and no one would ever think they'd been replanted.' Forrest shrugged broad shoulders. 'Aside from those things, it was a guess. Dusty Froman would use a place about like this. I can't exactly explain what I mean by that, except to tell you I knew him fairly well.'

Murph sat on the ground counting the little doeskin bags. Once, the moon sprang from behind a pale cloud and dumped milky light straight down. When that happened the broken bag showed a writhing, golden sheen and Murph clapped his hat over it lifting his big head and peering suspiciously all around.

'We got to get the hell away from here,' he whispered. 'Go get the horses, Forrest.'

The other man walked away without a word. He was in sight all the way to the corral, but he still could have jumped astride and plunged down into one of the nearby passes very simply. He didn't do that, though; he returned and handed Murphy Crail the reins to his animal. Murph was still having trouble overcoming his awe.

'Should've brought saddlebags,' he muttered.

'You didn't believe we'd find anything,' said Forrest.

Murph stood up, thick, oaken legs wide-planted in a protective stance. 'You're right, Forrest,' he conceded. 'I'm not going to argue that with you.' He grinned slightly. 'And I'm still having trouble believing it's happened.'

They had trouble getting their gold horde ready to be moved. It wasn't just heavy as lead, it was also bulky and awkward to handle. But they transported it for the best of all reasons—because they had to

On the ride back Murphy began to lose that paralysis of astonishment somewhat. He said, after they were well

75

away from Froman's camp, 'Forrest; I pulled a dumb stunt back there, sending you after the horses.'

The prisoner shook his head. 'Not dumb, exactly, because I had no idea to make a break for it. Not yet, Sheriff. Not until someone tries to send me to Montana in chains. Then I'll make my break.'

'Then it could be too late,' suggested Crail.

Forrest said he knew this to be true, more than likely, then he also said: 'It's a genuine squeeze, Sheriff. If I wait and find out they really mean to try me up in Montana, I'll probably get shot trying to break away. If I'd made a break back there—and they *didn't* want me up in Montana—I'd then be a fugitive from Humboldt County law, and I'd have to be lookin' over my shoulder for the next ten years or so.' Forrest looked around. 'That's quite a spot for a man to be in, isn't it?'

'Tell me something,' said the sheriff. 'If I was to set you loose on bond would you try to get away before I heard from Montana?'

'No.'

'Then you're loose on bond,' pronounced Murphy.

'How much bond?'

'Damned if I know. Tell you what: Your horse an' outfit at the liverybarn'll be your bond.'

Morgan Forrest grinned. It was unusual to say the least, but then genuine justice usually was; it was the law that never deviated from being dull, colourless, often quite blind and even more often guided by faulty logic.

They reached town only several hours ahead of sun-up and Murphy Crail showed Forrest the unusual steel box built into the floor under Murphy's desk. 'There's quite a story goes with this safe,' said Murphy. 'One time a band of renegades chased gold miners all the way southward from the Umpqua River country tryin' to overhaul 'em, massacre 'em, and get their gold-dust. They never caught 'em, but it was mighty close several times. One of the miners was the first sheriff hereabouts; that steel safe was hauled all the way up here from Frisco at his personal expense. He became the banker of Humboldt County and no one's ever even tried opening this thing.'

They got their gold locked into the safe, Murphy's desk shoved back over the false door, then sat a moment to relax. Murph said, 'You know what I think, Forrest? I think you were more right than you knew when you said if we didn't get the cache tonight we'd never get it. The reason I figure it like that is because if you noticed those droopy choke-cherries, so would someone else.'

Morgan shrugged. This was speculation. It could be very correct and it also could be very incorrect; but regardless, there wasn't a whole lot of sense at this time making these pointless speculations. He said, 'I'll turn in,' and arose to go into the cell.

Forrest nodded, watched the swarthy man depart, close the door after himself, and moments later also clang closed his cell door. Forrest made a smoke and cocked up his feet on the desk. He too was sleepy, but the last of his excitement hadn't quite died away so he felt fidgety and restless. He even moved the desk and made sure he'd spun the dial on that safe. After that he finished his smoke and fell asleep in his chair without any inkling this might happen.

When he awakened it was full daylight, the town was alive and quietly going about its affairs, and the same yapping dog which had awakened Murph also evidently awakened Morgan Forrest because he could be heard splashing water in the washbasin beyond the cell-room door.

Murph's palm grated over beard-stubble when he rubbed his jaw. He ignored that, waited until Forrest came out, then suggested they go for breakfast. They did.

Moreover, it was so late when they arrived at the restaurant they had the whole counter to themselves. The caféman blinked at sight of Forrest Morgan without manacles, but regained his composure at once and acted as though he hadn't been surprised.

After eating they went down to the liverybarn to check on their horses. Phil Barker was down there loudly arguing with an indignant liveryman. When Murph walked in both Barker and the liveryman turned, went through the identical blinking routine as the caféman, then Phil said, 'Murph; he's trying to make out that doggoned horse that was shot up near Froman's camp was worth a hundred dollars. Why; that cussed nag wasn't just long in the tooth, he was rickety in the joints and—'

'Sheriff,' exploded the liveryman. 'It ain't so. That horse wasn't no colt, true enough, but he was one of the best livery critters in m'string. He made me on an average of five dollars a week, an' he had a lot of good years in him. Now I figured it up an' accordin' to my calculations he'd make me—'

'You doggoned highwayman,' roared Phil. 'At five bucks a week, to make you a hundred dollars he'd have to live to be—'

'Sheriff,' bellowed the liveryman, over the saloonman's shouting. 'I wouldn't have tooken less, if someone'd come to buy that horse. Not a cent under a hundred dollars. So why should I take less now?'

Murph scowled at them. 'I'm not deef,' he snapped. 'And I'm not a judge. Phil; for gosh sakes—that lousy horse saved your bacon. What more could you ask?'

This altogether different train of thought caught Barker unprepared. He closed his mouth, thought a moment, then rammed a hand into his trouser pocket glaring at the liveryman. 'On that basis,' he said,

'Murphy's right. Otherwise I'd let you sue me 'till the cussed cows came home, because thirty-five bucks would be a fair price for that rack of bones.' Phil counted out one hundred dollars and handed it over. He then pushed what remained of his wadded bills back into his pocket and very pointedly turned his back on the liveryman, who went stamping away not quite as indignant as before, but still plenty nettled.

Phil's rancour died slowly. 'How come you let Forrest out?' he asked, ready for another argument.

'He posted bail,' stated Murph. 'His horse an' outfit.'

There wasn't anything here Phil could pick an argument about; in fact he began to look grudgingly pleased. 'Then let's go up to my place and have a drink,' he said, and went stamping out of the liverybarn.

They hadn't been inside more than a few minutes when Paul Standish entered and said he'd just seen Cap Bozeman's rig turn in down at the liverybarn. He said this before Forrest turned and Paul saw his face. At once he asked the same question Barker had asked.

'Murphy; how come you let him out?' Murph patiently explained and Standish came forward, reached for the beer Phil had automatically set in front of him, and thoughtfully sipped. He and Phil exchanged a knowing look. Nothing more was said of Cap Bozeman's return to Douglas. In fact, for several moments nothing was said at all. Phil offered to set up another round but got no takers, after all, it was still early morning. So Phil drew a glass for himself, leaned on the bar in front of Forrest and said, 'Now you're out Now when do you want us to have the gather made and where do you figure to enter the mountains with 'em?'

Before Forrest could answer Murphy Crail spoke up. 'He's not taking your herd out of here until he's been tried and acquitted, Phil. That's the law; a man on bail just can't go traipsing out of the country.'

'Sure he can,' retorted the saloonman. 'He'd forfeit his bail, of course, but hell, Murph, Paul an' Cap an' I'd buy him another outfit.'

'No!' exclaimed big Murphy Crail, striking the bar with his fist. 'He stays right here in town until he's tried.'

Paul Standish moved in to head off the fierce argument about to erupt. 'That's fair enough, because Cap brought back a circuit judge with him from down at Mattole.'

Murphy looked levelly at Paul. 'So that's where he went. And you two knew it, didn't you?'

'What's wrong with that?' asked Standish, surprised. 'You want the man tried too, don't you?'

Murph continued to balefully regard Standish. Eventually he said, 'Sure I do. Only it wouldn't have hurt if you'd told me what Cap was up to. After all, I'm not your enemy, Paul.'

Phil mumbled: 'Sometimes I wonder about that,' but when Murph swung his shaggy head, Phil grabbed up their glasses and stepped away to refill them.

Morgan was amused; it showed in the strong, tough lift of his lips and in the quiet brightness of his dark eyes. When their beers came back he raised the glass saying, 'Here's to the future,' and drank.

The others also drank. They were still hunched over Phil's bar when Cap Bozeman strolled in looking no more rumpled than usual, and with a sly twinkle in his eyes. Barker drew off another glass and set it solidly where Bozeman edged in against the bar.

'Glad to see you made it all right,' said Phil.

Cap twinkled them all a merry look. 'No trouble at all. The judge is down at the rooming-house gettin' cleaned up. He said he'd look you up directly, Murphy, then hold court in the morning.' He drank, used the back of one hand to swipe away foam from his moustache and looked around again. 'Anything new happen since I been away?'

They told him of the attack upon Barker and Standish and how it was resolved. Phil growled that this was the only time in his life he'd ever had to save his own hide then pay a hundred dollars to a horsethief for the privilege.

Cap then said, 'Down at Mattole I told the sheriff what we had goin' on up here an' he was right interested. He said there'd been inquiries made in a routine way to his office from Frisco a couple months back about any strangers passin' gold coins.'

They discussed this briefly, then Murph and Morgan Forrest walked out of the saloon leaving the other three still at the bar. On the plankwalk outside Murph said, 'If anyone finds out where that damned gold is, it's going to get kind of warm around here.'

'No one'll find out,' Forrest replied. 'You won't tell and neither will I. All they'll find is that hole under the choke-cherry bush. That ought to discourage 'em from lookin' any further.'

They went down to the jailhouse, stopped off for some food at the restaurant, and took it to the other prisoners. 'Dobe Hill's broken leg was giving its owner plenty of anguish. The flesh had swollen until the splints were half buried in it. Hill wouldn't touch the food; his face was beaded with sweat from the pain. Murph went to his desk and brought back what remained of that whiskey they'd drunk the day before. Hill gulped it down and lay back on his pallet panting.

Stan Foley ate both breakfasts and afterwards placidly made a cigarette. He seemed, if not exactly contented, then at least resigned. Murph told Foley to call him if Hill got any worse, and went back out into the office with

Morgan Forrest. 'That leg looks bad,' he confided. 'I hope to hell there's no infection.'

Forrest didn't think there was. 'They always puff up like a flour sack when they're busted like that. He'll be all right; just give him a couple of weeks.'

'I wonder,' muttered Murph, 'what the judge'll give him?'

'I'm more interested in what the judge'll give *me*,' said Morgan Forrest.

Chapter Ten

The circuit judge was a short, slightly pop-eyed man in his late fifties who seemed quite seasoned at his work. In fact, when he convened court the following day just before high noon, he took Murph aside and told him what he intended to do.

'One witness and no record, Sheriff, both point to the advisability of acquittal on the grounds of self-defence. Of course the fact that Froman is—or was—the man who robbed that San Francisco bullion coach won't make his killer a villain in the eyes of the law. But,' and here the judge waggled a finger under Murphy's big nose, 'there's also the possibility, as you told me last night, of this man Forrest being wanted up in Montana, so I'm going to recommend he be held in official custody until you hear about this one way or the other. How does that sound to you?'

Murph wasn't pleased, exactly. 'I thought you could only try a man for one crime at a time,' he mumbled.

'That's right,' exclaimed the judge. 'And that's all I'm going to do. What made you believe otherwise?'

'Well; you just said you'd order him back into custody, Judge.'

'Certainly. But I'm not trying him for something that might've happened in Montana. All I'm doing is making certain he'll be on hand when Montana lets you know whether he's wanted there or not.'

Murph scratched the end of his nose looking dubious. 'Judge; we got a problem here in Douglas. No ships have come to take off the cattle. The ranchers are bad off financially. In fact there probably isn't a thousand dollars

83

in cash among them all, and the folks who've been advancin' credit are just about up against it.'

'That's unfortunate,' said the judge a trifle impatiently. 'but what's it got to do with your prisoner or with me?'

Murphy told him. 'Forrest can trail their herds through the mountains. He's the only man around who's made that trip recent enough to know the way. And he happens to also be a drover by trade.'

The judge leaned back and tapped lightly upon his desk top. 'I see. In other words, you want Forrest turned loose so he can head up a cattle drive.'

'Yes.'

The judge grappled silently with his own predicament. 'And suppose Forrest *is* wanted in Montana—after he's clean out of your jurisdiction?'

Murph glumly nodded. He'd known this question would be thrown at him. 'I don't know,' he replied candidly. 'I could get his word to return, maybe.'

His Honour was wry about that. 'It would be putting a considerable strain on a man's word, wouldn't it, Sheriff, when by returning he might be sticking his neck into a noose?'

Murphy nodded glumly again. He could think of several excellent arguments favouring the release of Morgan Forrest, but they weren't likely to find much sympathy in a man whose mind had been trained in legalities. The best argument favouring Forrest's release from custody had to do with his help in locating and rehiding the cache of gold coin, and of course His Honour was certainly entitled to know about that, but Murph held off on the excellent grounds that what others did not know wasn't likely to cause anyone in Douglas City any trouble.

He sighed. 'Judge; what about those other two; the ones who tried to kill Barker and Standish?'

His Honour was just as candid about this case too. 'I'll acquit them too.'

Murph jumped as though stung. 'You'll *what?*'

'Acquit them, Sheriff. What else can I do? Those men were justified in believing they were under attack. What they did, obviously was committed in the belief they had to defend themselves.'

Murph was scandalized. He went back and sat down and let the judge call his court to order, proceed to personally conduct all cross examination and courtroom interrogation, then banged his gavel down and pronounced Morgan Forrest free of any charges levied against him on the grounds of self-defence as sworn to by Phil Barker and the defendant himself, then banged his gavel once more and called for Stan Foley and Adobe Hill to be brought forth.

Hill couldn't make it and was excused. Foley's story was straightforward and without embellishments. He looked the judge straight in the eye as he related how he and his partner had watched Barker and Standish skulking through the twists and turns among the Bald Hills as though stalking them—which Phil admitted red-faced was true—and how he and Hill decided they had to protect themselves against would-be bushwhackers, and proceeded to do so.

The only deviation came when Phil asked about that hundred dollars he'd paid for the dead horse; he was of the opinion that the man who'd killed the cussed beast should have to pay for it. The judge thought differently. In his best legal prose he said, 'Mister Barker; *you* rode that horse up there. I grant you Mister Hill shot the horse. But he was less at fault for that, thinking as he thought at the time—that you were trying to ambush him—than you were, for taking the animal up there in the first place, then proceeding not to approach openly and frankly, but used that horse to try and sneak up on the camp site. The responsibility for that dead horse, therefore, rests exclusively with you.'

Phil was disgusted, although he didn't look as though the decision actually surprised him at all.

Then the judge banged his gavel again, and said, 'With respect to these two matters, it is the opinion of this court that the men Hill and Foley be released from official custody at once. And that the man Forrest be held *in* custody pending notification by the Montana authorities whether or not he's wanted in that Territory for additional crimes.'

The gavel came down hard, with absolute finality. His Honour looked at the astonished faces gazing up at him, arose, gathered his papers and walked out of the room by a side door. Murphy, who had known this was coming, sat moodily waiting for the indignation to burst.

It did. Phil and Cap Bozeman jumped up. Paul Standish, sitting with his wife Annie, paled but made no outward demonstration of the way he obviously also felt.

Phil leaned down. 'Murph; what the devil's wrong with that judge? We got to have Forrest free to take the herds out.'

Crail turned, uncomfortable in the face of the indignation around him. People were filing out of the room heading for the roadway. They muttered back and forth a little, making a low droning sound as they shuffled away.

'That's the law,' muttered Murph unhappily. 'I tried to explain before court convened you fellers needed Morgan to get the cattle through the mountains.'

'He didn't care?' asked Phil, shocked at this possibility of callousness.

'Well; he didn't say whether he cared or not, Phil,' mumbled Sheriff Crail, and stood up. 'I'll tell you what;

I'll go down to the rooming-house and try again.'

Cap Bozeman's normally serene countenance looked a little antagonistic. 'Murph,' he said softly. 'I explained all about our trouble getting the cattle out, on the drive up here. Of course the judge never said anything one way or another, but still an' all, I figured he'd be a reasonable man and—'

Crail started shaking his head 'Cap; I've been around 'em before. They only think *Law*; what's got to be done accordin' to the written statutes.' Murphy raised and dropped his big shoulders and turned to march back outside.

Cap and Phil turned to where Morgan Forrest was standing patiently behind them, looking on and listening. Cap said, 'M'boy; it's just a technicality. I'll go down to the liverybarn with you, then we'll sort of take a sashay out and tell the rangemen to commence gatherin' the herds. We'll have them drifted over near the foothills where—'

Forrest said, 'You know better, Mister Bozeman. I'm not going outside the law. I told you fellers that before. When Sheriff Crail tells me I'm off the hook, I'll help you deliver your herd to the San Joaquin country. Not otherwise.'

Forrest also walked out. That left only two men in the room. Phil and Cap Bozeman. Phil glared after the departing man and started to swear, but Cap rubbed his palms together and said, 'Shhhh. Quit usin' that kind o' language, Phil. You heard him—he said he'd help us deliver the critters. Didn't you hear that? Well; that's the first really encouragin' word I've heard in a week from anyone. Now let's move on from there.'

'How?' growled the saloonman. 'Maybe Forrest is willin', but what about that shrimp of a judge?'

Cap avoided this, probably because right at the moment he had no logical solution. He took Barker's arm and started away. 'What we need,' he confided to the shorter, heavier man, 'is a good cool drink.'

Barker went along, but he was still angry. 'And the doggoned pint-sized caterwauler set those two loose who liked to killed Paul and me. Now by grabs, Cap, if that's how the law works, I prefer somethin' different.'

'Such as?'

Phil didn't know. 'Well; somethin' anyway. Maybe like the vigilance committee we used to have back in the early days.'

'You know a darned sight better'n that,' stated Cap Bozeman. 'Those committees weren't even good when there was nothing else. Now let's get that beer and cool off a mite.'

It was easier for Cap and Phil to find solace at Barker's bar than it was for Murphy and Forrest Morgan, sitting over in the jailhouse office. Forrest was resigned, but at the same time he wasn't at all pleased. He put it this way: 'I understand why he did that, being a judge and having law enforcement in mind, but what I told you about my cousin's death was the plain truth.'

'I know that,' muttered Murphy. 'I knew it the minute I heard what you and Froman said to one another before you killed him. It's not what *you* said; it's what *Froman* did. He knew exactly why you were over there to kill him across the road. A man don't need a whole lot better proof than that. Yet a judge can't go on things like that.'

Forrest crossed his legs and gloomily regarded the scuffed toes of his boots. 'There *is* a way,' he said quietly. 'Bring him over here, show him the gold and explain to him how you got it. That ought to make him at least agree to me being free on bail long enough to get those cattle through the mountains.'

'Yeah,' agreed Murph, squirming a little on his chair. 'I've pondered that. An' I reckon he wouldn't say

The Bald Hills

anything, at least until he got back down south to Frisco—but suppose I'm wrong; suppose he gets carried away or just plain lets it slip?'

Forrest didn't argue. He simply said, 'And I thought *I* was in a squeeze.' He regarded the unhappy big sheriff a moment. 'Are you elected to this job?' he asked, and when Murph nodded Forrest said, 'Not next term you won't be.'

Murph had also thought of that. "Be kind of hard goin' back to loggin' after this job,' he muttered, sounding filled with pity for himself. He shook out of it a moment later, arose and said, 'I'll be over at the rooming-house. We got to talk some sense into that doggoned judge.' He reached for the door and it swung violently open in his face, nearly striking him. Two rangemen burst in, sweaty and rumpled. One of them had an improvised bandage made of a blue bandanna handkerchief around his left arm up high.

Forrest and Crail looked up, startled. The wounded man said in an angry tone, 'Say, Sheriff; you got a law against folks shootin' other folks just because they're doin' their job?' He pointed to his injured arm. 'Pete an' me was riding north-west to check the drift up yonder in the Bald Hills, and without no warnin' at all, some danged brush-popper begun shootin' at us like we was an invadin' army or somethin'. Cut me a neat one right through the arm.'

Forrest unwound up to his feet. Murph, who knew these riders, said to the uninjured one, 'Pete; was it out by that camp the stranger had, where he made the little pole-corral?'

The man named Pete nodded vigorously and mopped sweat off his face. They were riders for Paul Standish. 'That's where it happened,' he exclaimed. 'We come to town to tell Paul only we couldn't find him, so we come

89

here. Now we got to go down to the liveryman an' get Matt's hurt tended to.'

Forrest moved closer to peer at the injury. It wasn't bad, at all; the bullet had sliced though the cowboy's arm to the right of the bone. It wasn't even bleeding any more. But it would be as sore as a boil for a few weeks, and even more than that, the man who had it would be angry as a hornet until whoever had shot him had been either also shot, or at least brought to book.

'How many are up there?' Forrest asked, and both cowboys shook their heads.

'We never hung around to find out, after Matt got winged,' said the one called Pete. 'But I can tell you this much; it sounded like a regiment when them darned guns opened up.' Pete grimaced at Murphy Crail. 'Sheriff; what the hell's it all about? Why should anyone get so all-fired touchy just over a couple of riders doin' their chores, and how come so many fellers should be right there at the old camp site?'

Murphy avoided answering by asking a question instead. 'Did Miz' Standish say where Paul was?'

'Yeah. Out on the range somewhere.'

Murph stiffened. 'Go down an' get Matt's arm patched up,' he told the cowboys, and pushed them out the door, then he turned on Morgan Forrest. 'Paul might head up to the camp site too; he knows about the story of that damned gold, anyway.'

Forrest retrieved his hat from the bench he'd been sitting upon and followed Murph out of the office and down the walk towards the liverybarn. When he finally caught up he said, 'Listen; if it's a crew of them we'd be silly to try this by ourselves. We'd get the same reception that cowboy got.'

Murph hesitated, then nodded. 'All right. You go get us a couple of horses. I'll go round up a few men and meet you down there.'

They split up, Forrest heading for the liverybarn, Murphy Crail reversing himself and heading straight towards Phil Barker's saloon. On the way he passed Abe Sherman out front of the blacksmith shop and called for him to come along. Abe came, but he looked bewildered by the order.

Chapter Eleven

There were Cap Bozeman, Phil Barker who'd locked up his saloon to go along, Abe Sherman who'd locked up his blacksmith shop, Morgan Forrest and Murphy Crail. At the time that seemed to be enough. They could have dragooned Pete, the uninjured rider for Paul Standish but Murph didn't believe that necessary.

'There are five of us,' he told the others. 'That's enough to rout a whole nest of 'em.'

No one argued with this because only Crail and Forrest had heard Pete and Matt excitedly describe the number of men out at Froman's camp site. In fact they didn't discuss this at all as they left town in a lope, but instead talked of Paul's chances if he too, rode close enough to be attacked.

Phil Barker growlingly told them all that he wasn't going to pay for the livery horse he was riding this time, 'Because confound it all, I'm not doin' this voluntarily; this time I'm doin' it as a posseman for the cussed county.'

No one laughed although under other circumstances Cap Bozeman might have been amused.

They rode fast, impelled by the sense of urgency Murphy Crail inspired in them. Each man was armed with a Winchester as well as a belt-gun. Forrest had the same gun on his hip he'd used to kill Froman He was also riding his own horse and saddle. Abe, like Phil Barker, didn't own a horse of his own and was mounted on a livery animal.

By the time they got within sight of the Bald Hills the sun was slanting away from them. It was a pleasant day without much heat; a little salt-scented breeze was running overhead, almost spent after its long inland journey.

When they left behind the last large trees and started through the rolling grassland, Murphy slowed to a fast walk and sent Phil on ahead to the heights, figuring that in this way there'd be no ambush.

Cap got saddle-sore and rode some of the way standing in his stirrups. The others might have ragged him about that, but not under these circumstances.

Phil signalled, pointing almost due west. They saw but did not comprehend and Phil was too far away atop a high knob to be heard if they'd shouted up at him. The solution was obvious: Murph headed for the nearest tall hill and angled around toward the top of it.

What they eventually saw was a field of armed riders paralleling them, heading in the same northerly direction towards the camp site. Phil swore. Cap Bozeman, not at all likely to become disgruntled nor profane, said simply, 'The question is: Are those the same men who fired on Paul's riders, or is this another, fresh bunch of treasure-hunters?'

Murph, studying the course, the gait, and the general terrain, said, 'We'll cut them off from the camp, whoever they are.'

After dropping down off their hill and beckoning for Phil to rejoin them, Morgan Forrest took the lead and kept his horse at a fast walk all the way. He didn't slow his pace until he turned to ask Murph to send someone aloft again to see if they were athwart the route of the strangers. Phil turned without a word and pushed his livery animal back up another bald hill. This time though he had enough presence of mind to approach the top-out from the west, which was the far-side where he wouldn't be readily visible. He sat his saddle for a long while just below the rim, then turned and rode back down again to report.

'Dead ahead,' he said to Forrest. 'There's a fork in the

trail up ahead. Stick to the right-hand path an' it'll bring us across the creek and into some bushes right smack-dab where those men are goin' to also cross.'

Forrest nodded and moved out again briskly. Murph said, 'How many, Phil?'

The saloonman's answer came straight back. 'Six. And they're not from around here. I could tell that from the way their leader keeps looking around for his trail.'

Murph caught up with Morgan Forrest and these two kept the lead until they reached the creek. Around them on all sides were more of those low, fat little hillocks. Cap and Abe looked uncomfortable about being down in the shadowy crevice with higher slopes on all sides. These two were older; they'd seen the disasters which accrued to early-day settlers who let themselves be caught down in low places like this when the redskins were on the high ground.

The tangles of scrub brush on both sides of the creek were no more than man-high. This posed a problem of what to do with their horses, whose heads stuck higher in the air than the underbrush. Murph solved this speedily by detailing Abe to take the animals on around the nearest slope out of sight.

The remaining four men then slipped ahead, got set in the bushes, and waited, carbines in hand, heads cocked to pick up the first sounds. When Forrest finally signalled to the others from his hiding place, those oncoming riders weren't more than a hundred yards away streaming down off the little hill at their back, heading straight for the creek where four armed men crouched waiting.

Murph got a good look at the leader. He was a bullish, black-bearded man wearing a checkered woollen shirt open half way down. Murph straightened up slightly at sight of this man, then he looked left and right to make certain his companions were in place, and when the black-bearded rider came up close, Murph stepped out

94

with his cocked carbine trained on the bearded man's chest.

'Hello, Frank,' he said.

The bearded man yanked his horse back in sharp astonishment. He'd been lounging along obviously suspecting nothing. The other riders crowded up and owlishly peered down where Murphy Crail stood. Their leader eventually recovered from his surprise and squinted hard. 'Murph. . .?' he said.

'Yeah. 'County sheriff, Frank.'

The big, bearded man settled back in his saddle. 'I heard you went to work at that,' he said in a booming-deep voice. 'What you pointin' that gun at me for, Murphy?'

'There's been a shooting, Frank. I want to look at your guns.'

Frank's dark eyes drew out narrow. 'We didn't shoot no one, Murphy. We just rode down from our loggin' camp before sun-up this morning.'

'What for, Frank?'

'Well . . . It's a sort of secret, Murph.'

'Not any more it isn't,' said Crail. 'And Frank; there's no hidden gold.'

The men with Frank leaned forward to hear better after Murphy said that. They were loggers from their flannel and wool shirts to their spiked loggers' boots. They were muscular, rough men with the scent of pine-sap about them. They had personal bundles tied to their saddles holding food. Otherwise, they seemed to be exactly what Frank had just said they were; men who'd only just recently arrived in the Bald Hills.

Murphy called over his shoulder to his companions. When they too stepped forth with cocked carbines, the lumbermen watched with grave eyes. Black-bearded Frank said, 'Murph; we never shot no one. I just told you—'

95

'The guns,' said Murphy. 'Hand these men your guns.'

Cap, Morgan, and Phil Barker went ahead to take the guns which were handed to them, sniff the barrels and examine the chambers. None of them showed any sign of having recently been fired. Or if such had been the case, the weapons had subsequently been well cleaned and reloaded to leave no trace of it.

Murph said, 'This is Frank Carleton; he and I used to log together several years back.'

The possemen nodded non-committally. They had already sized-up Frank and his companions as loggers, and rough-tough men, which their breed usually was. In fact, which their breed had to be if they remained loggers.

When the guns had been handed back Frank said, 'Murph; what did you say about there ain't no gold?'

'That's right, Frank. There's no gold at the camp you're heading for. Who told you otherwise?'

Frank turned in his saddle. The other mounted men also turned to study a thickly built blond man who looked uncomfortable under all those staring eyes. The blond man said, 'I run onto a pair of riders last night headin' up-country. They told me a feller had cached a big haul of gold down here. One of 'em said he got shot in the leg for tryin' to find it and now they were leavin' it to whoever got down here first. They said there was others after it—including you, Sheriff—and they said—'

'Hill and Foley,' growled Phil Barker. 'That's what we get for lettin' that lousy judge set those two loose. Now look what almost happened.'

Murphy explained about the injured man and his companion. The loggers turned crestfallen. The big blond man swore, but more, it appeared, in relief at being vindicated for his part in the fiasco at the end of their long ride, than in actual disappointment.

Frank Carleton eased out of his saddle and stretched powerful, thick legs which had never been developed with a view towards employing them straddling horses. The others also got down. Cap went back to get Abe and the horses. When he returned Murphy Crail was explaining about the shooting of Paul Standish's cowboy, and what the possemen were doing now—searching for Standish and heading towards Froman's camp. When Murph asked the loggers if they'd care to help in the search, Frank Carleton shrugged.

'We rode ourselves sore gettin' this far,' he grumbled, looking around at his companions for confirmation, 'we might as well ride a little farther.'

The other loggers agreed, and turned back to climb into their saddles again. Murph and his possemen also got astride. The entire party then splashed across that little creek and strung out behind Carleton, Forrest, and Sheriff Crail. They were by this time not more than two miles south and west of the camp site.

Phil went ahead to the higher places as before, scouting. That little salt-air breeze died, and heat built up down in the shallow canyons, but it wasn't a hot, dry heat and neither men nor horses suffered from it in the slightest. More than anything else, the loggers were disgruntled. Frank kept asking about the story of Froman's buried treasure. Murph skirted the truth as wide as he dared without telling Carleton an outright lie; it wasn't easy because Carleton persisted in knowing all there was to know. In the end Murph, with Morgan's amused glance upon him, said, 'Now I'm not sayin' there wasn't a cache, Frank. All I'm sayin' is that with all the diggers around lookin', it sure isn't there any more.'

'Well; but how can you be sure of that?' persisted the tenacious logger. 'Murph; unless you dug that gold up yourself you can't be—'

'Hold it,' called Cap Bozeman. 'Phil's signalling.'

97

D

They halted. Barker was making some frantic motions from atop a nearby slope, gesturing westward and waving his hat with unintelligible but desperate motions. Cap said something was wrong; that Phil didn't get that excited very often. Barker then spurred his horse down off the slope with a recklessness which held them all spellbound, expecting him to go end over end any moment. He didn't though, and even when his horse stumbled as it regained flat country, Phil held its head up, the animal regained its balance, and came shooting straight down through the maze of shallow canyons towards them.

'I seen him,' he yelled. 'I saw Paul. But there's a bunch of fellers slippin' around him on all sides down in these lousy canyons. He's headin' straight for the camp without even knowing they've got him under their guns. Come on; I'll show you the way!'

'Hold it,' bawled Murphy as Barker yanked his horse around. 'Hold it, Phil. How many are stalkin' him?'

'Looks like maybe eight or ten,' responded the excited saloonman. 'Come on, Murphy; we got half again as many!'

Barker hooked his livery animal and sent it rushing down through the westerly maze. Behind him the others, caught up by Phil's excitement, also hooked their animals. Even the loggers were anxious and rode hard, forgetting their aches and pains.

The sun was no longer overhead, which was a kind of blessing. Shadows fell first into the narrow, shallow canyons, which cooled them off immediately. Once, they came whipping around a slope and rode head-on into a band of resting cattle. The horses slammed back hard in one direction, the startled cattle sprang up and exploded in the other direction. Phil kept spurring and rode right through them. He had his carbine in his right hand, his reins in his left hand. He acted as though he'd scarcely

98

even seen the astonished cattle.

Murph and Morgan Forrest were part way back in the hastening file of riders. There were loggers and townsmen behind them. Up front, behind Phil Barker, rode Abe Sherman looking as though he wished he weren't up there.

They were getting closer to the camp in one sense—at least they were heading north-westerly instead of due westerly—but in another sense they were losing ground by not staying to the north. Not that it mattered; perhaps only the loggers were still dreaming of gold. Murphy and Morgan certainly weren't; they knew for a fact no gold was still at Froman's camp site. Phil and Cap, as well as uneasy Abe Sherman, weren't thinking of gold at all. They were striving hard to reach Paul Standish in time to prevent murder.

They made it.

Phil suddenly rushed around a slope and came almost face-to-face with a mounted man riding carefully down the same little draw. This man had a Winchester across his lap and was obviously being very careful to make no more noise than he could help. He was one of the stalkers who were fanning out to surround and overwhelm Paul Standish. The second he saw Phil he raised the carbine. But as more and more fiercely armed men charged up behind Barker, the stranger's eyes opened wider and wider, and he lowered his gun again for the very excellent reason that if he shot Phil Barker, he was going to get cut to pieces by all those other grim-faced men coming up behind him.

Phil roared at the stranger. 'Damn you, drop that gun!'

The man dropped it.

Chapter Twelve

There were eleven of them surrounding one bewildered man in a canyon too narrow for all of them to get close to their captive. He looked into their faces once, and after that directed his attention to the man with the badge on his shirt.

'Who are you?' Murph asked, 'And what are you doing here riding around with a Winchester in your hand?'

The man said, 'Just travellin' through, Sheriff,' and offered a greasy smile. 'Headin' for the coast, y'know, to maybe find work down-country a ways an'—'

'You're a lousy liar, mister,' growled Phil Barker. He poked the unarmed man hard with his carbine-barrel. 'Why are your friends tryin' to get around that feller on the hilltop out there?'

'That? Oh; well y'see we was just figurin' he might be a highwayman or somethin'. It pays to be right careful in country like this. Now me'n my friends back there—we number right close to the same number as you fellers, and we got plenty guns an' ammunition.' The stranger's voice firmed up as though by listening to his own veiled warning, it made him braver. 'You boys harm me an' them others'll come down here like a pack of wolves.'

'Shut up,' growled Frank Carleton, glaring at the stranger with obvious disgust.

Phil was anxious again; they'd wasted a minute or two with the stranger. Cap leaned, whispered something to Murph then rode on around the stranger as though going on up the canyon. He then turned quickly and struck hard. The stranger's hat fell and he followed it straight down to the ground. Cap put up his pistol.

Murph jerked his head at Phil to lead out again. They

rode carefully around the unconscious man eyeing him but not with pity, only with hard interest. There were still seven more like him somewhere up ahead, and not too far ahead at that.

A gunshot sounded. The report seemed to come from all directions at once. Murph hauled down to a sliding halt and called for the others to do likewise. Then they sat. There could be nothing more unnerving in a canyon than just one gunshot. Because it was rarely expected, it was almost impossible to pin-point. They sat and waited for the second shot, and if it hadn't come they'd have been more confused than ever, but it came, sharp and snarling.

Murph pointed northward. Phil nodded and led out again. They made their way up along the slopes ahead towards the more northerly country. Eventually, if they'd kept in that direction, they'd have reached the limits of the Bald Hills where dark forest began, but they only went up as far as the hilltops, and halted up there to watch a number of men closing in upon a solitary rider roughly in the centre of their surround.

'Got him neat as a fly in a spider's trap,' said Cap Bozeman. 'And we got them the same way.'

Murph made his appraisals and sent them on their ways. He took Morgan Forrest and headed in a straight line for the broad low hilltop where the horsemen were cutting off Paul Standish. He made no move to keep out of sight now. He wanted to be seen and expected to be seen.

Morgan said, 'That's a rough-looking crew, Sheriff. Looks to be three rangeriders, a couple of wolfers, a trapper and that other one looks like some kind of feller from back in the Rockies with his hide shirt and braided hair. Maybe a 'breed.'

There was no denying that those men closing in on Paul Standish and thus far too otherwise occupied to look behind them, were as unlikely a collection of frontier specimens as could be rounded up in one place at one time.

'The legend of Froman's lousy gold sure got around,' growled Murphy. 'You know what I'm thinkin'? Well; I'm thinkin' that even if we put a notice in the San Francisco and Reno newspapers that there isn't any gold, I'll still be having these doggoned trigger-happy types riding through my county for the next year or two.'

'You will,' agreed Morgan Forrest. 'But if you'll pass the word around that no one, particularly the rangeriders out here are to interfere in any way, or even ride over to be friendly, I reckon in time it'll be forgotten.'

'I was too late for the gold rush,' said Murph, watching Paul Standish's captors tighten their circle until they they had him tightly boxed in, 'but by golly seeing all these men making fools of themselves makes me believe it's just as well as I didn't see it.'

Up ahead, just short of stopping close to Standish, one of the bristling group of motley strangers hooted and turned his horse towards Murphy and Morgan Forrest. Morgan said, 'Well; they won't have to sneak up on us, but I sure hope those loggers and townsmen hold up their end of this. Otherwise we're going to be in some trouble, if I read those reactions down there right.'

The strangers had Paul now, but they were scarcely heeding him. Instead they'd come together facing Murph and Morgan, talking swiftly among themselves. Murph and Morgan kept right on riding towards them.

Eventually the strangers, seeing they weren't going to have to give chase or make other hostile demonstrations, sat watching. Just before Murph and Morgan got up close enough to halt, two of those rough-looking men dropped to the ground to hunker Indian-like, leaning upon their carbines. Then a third one did that. The first two were obviously wolfers—men who lived in the darkest forests and deepest canyons killing wolves for the bounty. The last one was perhaps a trapper, a squaw-man, or possibly a professional pot-hunter, one of those individuals who found a way to make killing game pay him a living by taking whatever he bagged down to the settlements to peddle.

It was the three unkempt, hard-faced rangemen, though, Murph and Morgan stopped in front of. Those strangers all saw Murph's badge. One of them leaned upon his saddlehorn, spat amber and said bitingly, 'Sheriff; you're out of your town, ain't you?'

Murph ignored the man to gaze past at Paul Standish. 'You all right?' he asked.

Paul nodded. The laconic man spat amber again, his face hardening towards Murphy. 'Sheriff; you ain't got good sense, ridin' up on us like you done. The odds're pretty big you won't ride away that easy.'

Murph didn't even ask them who they were or what they wanted. He simply said, 'There's no gold. That cache has been dug up, so you've had a long ride for nothing.'

A moon-faced man with thin features squeezed up in the centre said, 'Ain't much sign of others havin' been over there, Sheriff. Maybe you got a personal reason for not wantin' us around that camp, eh?'

'I've got a personal reason for not even wanting you in my county,' growled Murphy. 'Paul; ride through them and come on over here.'

'Hold it,' snapped the third rangeman, a cunning-eyed man with a muddy complexion and coarse-grained skin. 'He don't go nowhere, Sheriff, until we tell him to.'

Murph looked at the speaker. 'You want to ride to the jailhouse with me, mister?'

The cowboy smiled wolfishly showing bad teeth and mean lines in his face. 'You're big enough to make me do it,' he said, 'on foot an' without no gun, but that ain't

103

how it is right now, Sheriff.'

Murph nodded at Standish. 'Come on through them,' he repeated, addressing Paul Standish. 'They aren't going to do anything.'

Paul hesitated. One of the wolfers grunted and spat out a disgusted curse. He got slowly to his feet speaking to the muddy-faced cowboy without taking his eyes off the southerly lip of the flat place where they all stood. 'You better let him have his friend. I ought to get shot for not guessin' right off them two warn't alone. Look along the rim all around—carbines pokin' out at us. 'Be damned.'

Morgan and Murphy Crail waited, giving their adversaries time to see that in fact the wolfer had spoken the truth. They, who had surrounded Paul Standish the same stealthy way, had received the same kind of treatment.

The professional pot-hunter lifted his carbine, draped it across the crook of one arm and chuckled. He was genuinely amused. 'What a hell of a bunch of fellers we turned out t'be,' he said, still amused. 'It's a good thing they're whiteskins an' not redskins, or they'd have cut us down like wheat.' This man raised untroubled eyes to Murphy Crail. 'You win, Sheriff,' he said. 'You win by usin' one of the oldest tricks in the book—keepin' us occupied while your friends got into position.' The man's chuckle sounded again, but none of the others echoed it.

Murph raised a thick arm for the others to close in. They did, after a moment; came riding up onto the flat like hunters closing in upon a wounded buffalo, careful and deadly and thoroughly watchful.

The mean-faced cowboy swore with ardent feeling. Paul Standish pushed on through and lined himself up with Murphy and Morgan Forrest. He didn't look particularly upset by his experience; if anything he looked chagrined by it. He still had both his carbine and his Colt.

The loggers came in on two sides, the townsmen came in from the other two sides. When they halted the loggers dismounted with their guns, evidently preferring to fight, if that's what was coming, on foot. The townsmen sat still atop their indifferent animals, waiting for whatever the strangers cared to make out of this.

They made nothing out of it. The mean-faced rangeman was still cursing when one of his companions said, 'Shut up, Mike. That don't help none.' This man looked from their captors to Sheriff Crail. 'All right,' he said quietly, 'you pulled a ringer on us, so it's your play.'

'Where are you from?' asked Murphy.

'The San Joaquin country.'

'Where did you hear about this gold cache?'

'We didn't know nothin' about no cache, Sheriff; we heard over in the valley which way this feller'd went who robbed the Frisco coach, so we threw in together and come lookin' for him. Last night I went down to that log town south-west of these hills, listened around, picked up what'd happened and come back. Then we rode to the camp to commence huntin'.' The cowboy gave his head a little curt wag. 'It's no secret, if that's what you're getting' at, Sheriff. Folks are talkin' on both sides of the mountains. We're not the last ones you'll see come out of the forests lookin' for that feller an' that ten thousand in gold coin.'

'Which one of you shot a rangerider this morning?'

The men looked at one another, then looked at the ground or the sky or the rough-hewn western horizon, remaining silent. Murph waited, giving them plenty of time, then he said, 'I'll give you a choice; the man who shot that rider identifies himself an' comes back to town

105

with me—or the whole bunch of you ride back and get locked up. It's up to you; spit or close the window.'

The mean-eyed man squirmed in his saddle as his two mounted companions looked straight at him. Eventually he said, 'Well what did you expect me to do; them boys was riding straight at me, armed and—'

'Take him, Morgan,' said Murph coldly.

Morgan veered his horse over beside the mean-faced man, took away the guns and jerked his head. The cowboy started to protest. Morgan reached down and slapped the man's horse. It responded by walking over where Murph sat. No one said anything.

Murph studied the others. They were rough, rugged men down on their luck, every one of them. 'Go on back to the valley,' he told them. 'Keep out of this county. I'll remember each one of you. If I see you back here again for any reason you're goin' to be charged with being an accessory after the fact—which means you'll be jailed and tried for sittin' by and watchin' this man here try to commit murder, without makin' any attempt to stop it.' He lifted his rein-hand. 'And I'm tellin' you the honest truth—there is no cache around here. No hidden gold; no cache of any kind at all. Now move out, and head straight north back into those mountains. Don't stop and don't turn back. Get!'

The dismounted men silently clambered back across the leather. The others obediently turned without a word and headed away. For ten minutes Murph's companions sat watching, then the loggers stepped down and stood beside their horses, alternately considering the departing strangers and one another. Frank Carleton finally said, 'Murph; I got a feelin' about that cache, but that's all right. Aside from the law it's first come first served. Well; we got to head back.' He looked with distaste at his mount, sighed with loud resignation and got back astride. 'But you owe us a big dinner an' a few drinks if we're ever down t'Douglas City. All right?'

Murphy smiled and nodded. 'Just don't all you come at once,' he answered. 'I only make thirty dollars a month.'

Morgan was beside their prisoner. The rangeman looked about as dejected as a man could look. Cap Bozeman and Paul Standish were speaking softly. Phil Barker looked darkly at Paul.

'You doggoned idiot. You knew there might be trouble out here. What the devil got into you, anyway?'

Paul was embarrassed. 'Just lookin' at the livestock,' he said, turning his horse. 'And I'm obliged to you fellers. I had no idea that crew was out here until one of them shot and yelled for me to hold up. Then they all came easing over the sidehill like you fellers did.'

Murph and Morgan led off with the prisoner between them, heading down-country in the woolly late afternoon heading for town. For a long while there wasn't much said by any of them. Cap Bozeman eventually broke the silence by speculating on whether the judge would still be in town when they got back. Cap's thoughts were obvious; he was back to thinking about getting the cattle driven through the mountains again. It didn't occur to Cap, or to any of the others for that matter, that they might never get that drive under way because they wouldn't have to.

It was dusk before they reached Douglas, put up their animals and dispersed, Murph and Morgan taking the captive to jail. Phil Barker, walking part way with them, made a dour prediction.

'No sense to lockin' him up, Murph. That doggoned pipsqueak of a judge'll just set him loose anyway.'

But Murph threw his prisoner in a cell anyway, then he and Morgan went out to get something to eat.

107

Chapter Thirteen

The judge was still in town, very much so in fact. He'd no sooner heard of the sheriff's return with a prisoner than he hiked straight for the jailhouse, ignored Morgan Forrest and wanted to see the complaint filed against the captive.

Murph hadn't filled it out yet and said so. The judge looked down his nose at this. 'That's the first thing you're supposed to do,' he said sharply, and Murph, looking tired but at least full of supper had an answer for that.

'The first thing I do is catch my man, Judge. The second thing I do is lock him up. The third thing I do is get some supper. The fourth thing I do is get some rest. Then, the last thing I do is fill out those legal papers.'

'Well,' demanded the judge, 'do you propose to arraign him tomorrow? I can't waste much more time in Douglas, you know. I have a large territory to cover, a large calendar to keep up with.'

'Tomorrow'll be fine,' said Murph without any enthusiasm.

'What'll the charge be?'

'Attempted murder, Judge.'

'You have a witness?'

'Two; the man he shot in the arm and the man who was riding along when his friend got shot.'

'I see. Well; that's promising. And the prisoner; does he have any rebuttal-witnesses?'

Morgan's eyes twinkled at Murph from behind the judge's back. Any rebuttal-witnesses the prisoner might have had, were by now cursing their way empty-handed back through the mountains at the sheriff's orders.

Murph shook his head. 'Not a one, Judge.'

For a moment the jurist stood in thought, then he brightened as he said, 'Arraign him right after breakfast in the morning, Sheriff. Then I can leave Douglas before noon and be on about my duties with plenty of daylight to ride by.'

Murph got up nodding, opened the door for the judge and as the much smaller, older man was marching through, Murph said, 'Your Honour; don't call it justified this time.'

The judge turned with an indignant expression. 'Sheriff; justice is blind. We operate strictly by—'

'She sure as hell is, sometimes,' said Murphy, and eased the door closed.

Morgan laughed but Murph remained stony-faced. 'You want to bed down in the cell again tonight?' he asked the man who'd killed Dusty Froman. 'You could get a better room over at the rooming-house.'

'I've been returned to official custody,' replied Forrest, still amused. 'Anyway; this grey-bar hotel is a lot cheaper than the rooming-house.'

Murph left, didn't bother going up to Phil's place for a nightcap, and went to his room to get a decent night's sleep. He got it. He also got a surprise when he arose the following morning and went into the café for breakfast. The surprise had nothing to do with the fact that Morgan was there ahead of him chewing a shoe-sole piece of fried steak and washing as much of it as he could masticate down with black coffee. What surprised him was the corner table near the roadway window with its four leathery strangers. They wore deputy U.S. marshals' badges.

As Murph sank down beside Morgan, Forrest said, 'Well; that proves the road from San Francisco northward up to Douglas City is open to all kinds of travellers, doesn't it?'

Murph nodded at the caféman. He didn't have to order, breakfast always consisted of the same food: Fried beefsteak, black coffee, and a bowl of peaches; good substantial food. So good it lay in a man's stomach like a shot-pouch full of lead until near suppertime.

'They'll be after the gold,' said Morgan, watching Murph slyly study the federal lawman.

Murph nodded. 'They can have it too. I had a bad dream last night about someone finding the safe under my desk and getting it open.'

Morgan got a refill for his cup when Murph's breakfast came. 'That prisoner sure squawked this morning,' he said as Murph tore into his food. 'Seems he's been thinking, and his kind only thinks about one thing. He says you had no right to lock him up. He said he'll deny to high heaven he even saw those two cowboys yesterday, let alone took a shot at them.'

Murph went right on eating. He hadn't expected much else from the sly-eyed, mean-faced rangeman. It happened quite often. But Murph had a cure for it, too, so he went on placidly filling his stomach and only spoke after he'd shoved the empty plate from in front of him.

'Head for the jailhouse,' he told Morgan. 'I'll have a little talk with these federal men then be along.'

Morgan nodded, put some coins on the counter and left. Murph took his cup of coffee over, introduced himself and leaned on the wall eyeing the four federal officers. The oldest one said his name was Peterson. U.S. Deputy Marshal Carl Peterson from San Francisco. He introduced his companions then said they'd heard from the sheriff down at Mattole that a man named Cap Bozeman had ridden into Mattole looking for the circuit judge to take him north to try some man for the killing of another man named Froman.

Murph concurred with all this, then asked if Marshal

110

Peterson knew who Froman had been. Peterson's cool, assessing gaze looked straight up at Sheriff Crail. 'We know,' he said. 'That's why we're here, Sheriff. There's a little matter of ten thousand in gold coin Froman stole from a bullion coach. You got any idea what he did with it before he got himself killed?'

All four of those leathery faces looked inquiringly at Crail. He finished his coffee and put the cup aside. 'You boys expecting a hard hunt with a lot of digging?' he asked. 'If so, forget it; the money has been recovered and is in a safe place.'

Marshal Peterson's tight expression relaxed. 'See,' he said to the three younger deputy marshals. 'I told you all the way up the coast we might not have to stay up here more'n a day or two.'

The younger lawmen said nothing but they appeared just as relieved as Marshal Peterson obviously was. Then Murphy drew up off the wall and said, 'I'll be down at the jailhouse, when you're through breakfast,' and walked out of the café. He still had that prisoner to soften up, and he hadn't filled out the charges on the necessary forms yet.

When he got down there Cap Bozeman was talking with Morgan Forrest. Without hearing a word of it, Murph knew what Cap was discussing: His cattle drive though the mountains.

Murph closed the roadside door, said the U.S. deputies would be along shortly, and with a little quick nod at Cap, went into the back room where his cells were. He carefully closed the door at his back leading into the outer office.

The prisoner glared from a surly face and stood in the centre of his cell. 'I've got a right to see a lawyer,' he growled.

'We don't have one in Douglas City,' said Murph, almost cheerfully, and unlocked the cell door. 'In fact

111

we've never had one here, that I ever heard about.' He closed the cell door at his back and stood a moment sizing up the man called Mike. 'But you won't need one anyway,' he said in the same brisk, business-like voice, 'because the judge acts as interrogator. He asks questions and you answer them—after you've taken the solemn oath on the Bible to speak the truth.'

Mike was gazing straight at big Murphy Crail, an inkling of a suspicion in his mind, apparently, for he said, 'Now wait a minute, Sheriff; I thought them two cowboys was after me. I had a perfectly legitimate reason for what I done. You can't come in here and . . .'

Murphy removed his hat, placed it upon the bunk, and flexed his huge hands. The prisoner took an involuntary step backwards without attempting to finish what he'd been saying.

'I've got the same kind of reason for what I'm about to do, also,' said Murph, taking one big step forward. 'I want the truth here. Later, I'll expect you to tell it to the judge. And afterwards, when he's passed sentence an' I escort you out of the courtroom, you and I'll have another little set-to if you lied to His Honour.' Murph lifted his mighty arms. 'Well; what'll it be?'

'Honest,' bleated the rider, going back until his shoulders struck the log wall. 'I thought them two was. .'

'All right,' said Murph with resignation. 'You made your choice so now you'll get your medicine.'

'Wait,' gasped the cowboy. 'Hold it, Sheriff . . . All right; I'll tell the truth. We seen 'em comin' and figured they was after the cache too. We let 'em get close then let fly at 'em to chase 'em away. I shot a mite close is all. I. . .'

'You thought if you dropped one the other one would high-tail it and spread the word there were some diggers at the camp who'd fight,' stated Murph.

112

The cowboy nodded weakly.

Murph picked up his hat, dropped it on the back of his head and turned, walked out and turned back to lock the cell door. When he'd finished he said, 'Mister; that's exactly the story I want to hear you tell His Honour, an' if you fail me, remember what I said—after trial I'll walk outside with you.' He passed through into the front office and found the four iron-face federal officers there waiting for him. Cap Bozeman had gone but Morgan Forrest still sat relaxed and knowing, as Crail crossed to his desk and sat down He held out a huge hand towards Marshal Peterson. 'The badges are good enough but I want your other identification too.'

Peterson showed no annoyance. He handed over some papers, including a letter signed by the Governor of California directing the U.S. Marshal at San Francisco to make every possible effort to find out where the bandit had gone who'd stolen that money. Peterson said, of this letter, 'I brought it along in case you were interested in knowing what a furore that robbery caused.'

Murph handed back the papers and the letter. He looked at Morgan, then they both arose, grabbed the oak desk and heaved it sideways. Morgan lifted out the flooring and Murph got down to open the steel safe. Marshal Peterson and his companions looked on with surprise and interest. Even after Murph and Morgan had neatly stacked the little doeskin sacks on the floor, the federal lawmen continued to look surprised.

Carl Peterson finally went over, got down on one knee and began counting the little sacks. He said, 'How did you find it?' to Sheriff Crail.

Murph's lips lifted slightly as he dryly said, 'It wasn't very hard. I had a good guide, Marshal. It's all there except two hundred dollars. We figure Froman spent that over in the San Joaquin, which is what started all these manhunters arriving around the Bald Hills.'

113

Peterson told one of his men to bar the roadside door. After this was done he put the little sacks on Murphy's desk and stood gazing at them. His deputies crowded in to also stare. Finally, looking immensely pleased, Peterson said, 'Sheriff; by golly you've sure earned the reward.'

Murphy looked up. 'I didn't know there was a reward.'

'Ten per cent, Sheriff. That'll figure out to about a thousand dollars, depending on how short of ten thousand this turns out to be. We'll count it and give you a receipt, then we'll get on down south with it.' Peterson smiled; it was evidently an expression which came hard to him because it looked less cheerful than triumphant. 'Care to help us count?' he asked.

Murph shook his head. 'I'll leave Morgan here to help with that. I've got to take a prisoner across the road to the community building to be tried.' Murph raised his brows at Forrest. Morgan nodded, indicating he'd stay and assist with the counting. Murph then stepped to the back-room doorway and turned back to say, 'Marshal; I'm not telling you your business, but in your boots I wouldn't ride out of here in broad daylight with that gold.'

Peterson looked squarely back. 'Who knows we have it besides you and this man here?' he asked.

'No one. But believe me; since it came into the country there's been no end of strangers poking around looking for it.'

Peterson shrugged. 'Let 'em look. By supper time tonight it'll be so far down-country they couldn't catch up to us with wings.'

Murph went after his prisoner, took him out into the office and almost ran over the man when he stopped in mid-stride, staring over where all those little sacks were being emptied of their gold-shiny contents upon Murphy's desk for the money to be counted. Then the rangerider began to heartily curse. Murph gave him a rough shove towards the roadside door. 'Bar it after me,' he said, and left the building.

The sun was high, there was a promise of unusual heat in the air, people were busily going about their chores, and over in front of the little log building used for a courtroom when this was necessary, but which actually was the community fire hall, dance-hall, and gathering place, Paul Standish's two riders were standing with their employer and his prim wife. Also standing over there was His Honour, scowling impatiently at the face of a large gold pocket-watch.

Murph said, 'Move out,' to his prisoner, and laid a huge hand upon the man's shoulder. The cowboy obeyed, but he dragged his feet and when they were half across the roadway with those idlers over there watching, he turned his head, screwed up his thin features and asked a question.

'You had that gold all the time?'

'Not all the time,' Murphy replied. 'Just since night before last when we went out there an' dug it up. Now keep moving.'

'Well why the hell didn't you say so, Sheriff?'

'Because I didn't want you and your friends or anyone else busting into my jailhouse and trying to blow up that safe to get it.'

'Those U.S. lawmen: They goin' to take it away with them?'

'What do you care? You're not going to be able to do anything about it. Yes; they're going to take it back down to Frisco where it belongs.'

'Oh, Lord,' groaned the prisoner, and resumed his crestfallen walk over towards the courtroom where the others were finally filing on inside. Once more, just before passing on inside he said the same thing again.

'Oh, Lord.'

There were fewer spectators at this trial because fewer knew what had happened. Still; the room was half-full, and as far as Murphy Crail was concerned, that was plenty of visitors anyway; he was only interested in the judge, right now, and his prisoner.

Chapter Fourteen

There wasn't much deviation to this trial from the previous trials, except that near the end of it His Honour asked the prisoner point-blank if he'd meant to hit Paul Standish's rider when he fired at him.

This was where the prisoner hung fire. He looked from the judge down to where big Sheriff Crail was slouching in a chair, one hand to his face, his blue eyes fixed without wavering upon the prisoner's face, then the man nodded his head.

Standish and his cowboys exchanged a look. The wounded cowboy particularly, was pleased. His Honour reared back in his chair, lifted his gaze and said, 'Guilty as charged. This man will be remanded into the custody of Sheriff Crail to be transported to San Quentin Penitentiary there to commence at once serving a sentence of from one to five years for assault with the intention to commit great bodily harm.'

The judge struck with his gavel, hesitated a moment to return Murphy Crail's solemn look, then gathered up his papers, his gavel, and with enormous dignity, considering he wasn't much bigger than a half-grown girl, marched majestically out of the building.

Standish's wife said loudly enough to be heard over most of the room: 'It's getting so's a body's not safe in Humboldt County any more.' Murphy straightened in his chair, turned to see whether she'd been maligning him personally, met Paul's sheepish look, and arose to go over and take the prisoner in tow. As they were leaving, straggling out with the last of the spectators Paul sidled up and said, 'Murphy; you know how women are sometimes.'

117

Murph looked dour. 'No, Paul, I don't know. But I know how horses and dogs and men are, sometimes, an' when they get smart like that there's nothing to fetch 'em around so fine as a good swift kick in the belly when their backs are turned.' He then continued on outside.

When he ushered his prisoner back into the jailhouse those four deputy federal officers and Morgan Forrest had the money neatly stacked in its little pliable sacks, and were smoking, sitting easy around the office. Murph took his prisoner on through, locked him up and returned.

'How much?' he asked, looking at Morgan.

Marshal Peterson answered. 'Nine thousand and three hundred dollars, Sheriff, right down to the last dollar. How'd you come out with your trial?'

'Fine. He drew one to five for assault. It's not what I'd have given him, but then I'm not the judge either.'

As though on cue, the judge barged in. Murphy had neglected to bar the door from the inside and none of the others had moved to do it either. He started to speak, saw that money in its thick little stack, and apparently forgot what it was he was going to say. Then he looked around at all those badges, comprehending, and pointed.

'Is that the money everyone has been looking for, Sheriff?' he asked.

Murphy nodded, repeated the amount exactly as it had been told him, then said, 'You did a fair job on my prisoner this morning, Judge. If you'd care to step up the road with me I'd stand the first couple of rounds at Barker's saloon.'

'And leave this money lying on your desk, Sheriff?'

Murph looked down his nose. 'There are four U.S. lawmen here to guard it. And Morgan Forrest too. I think it'd be a sorry day for someone to walk in here with robbery in mind.'

118

The judge eyed Carl Peterson. 'Don't I know you?' he said.

Peterson shrugged. 'I've been around the bay area as a deputy marshal for seven years, Judge. We've probably met.' Peterson gestured. 'These are my deputies.' He then said, 'Judge; if you're planning on riding south today, you can come along with us. We'll be goin' the full distance back to Frisco.'

His Honour dwelt momentarily upon that offer then shook his head. 'No thanks, Deputy. I think under the circumstances a man might be a whole lot safer travelling alone—not with ten thousand dollars in gold.'

Peterson wasn't concerned. 'Suit yourself,' he murmured, and arose. 'But Judge; one favour: Don't mention what you've seen in here.'

His Honour looked indignant. 'Of course not, Deputy. After all I also serve the law.' He turned back to Murphy Crail. 'I came over to tell you that upon sober reflection I've decided to admit Mister Forrest to that bail you seemed to believe he's entitled to.'

Murph nodded. He'd already admitted Forrest to bail. 'Obliged,' he said impassively. 'See you again, Judge, if you're ever back this way.'

His Honour departed and right behind him went Carl Peterson looking thoughtful and grave as he headed for the liverybarn where his horse, and the mounts of his men, had been stabled.

Phil Barker came in later, after the sacks of gold money had been placed out of sight, and seemed surprised to find three youthful deputy U.S. marshals in Murphy's office. He hesitated to speak even when urged to do by Sheriff Crail.

Finally though he said, 'Murph; a stage just come in with a ship's captain on it. I know it's not important, but Cap an' Paul an' I figured it was worth lettin' Mister

Forrest know, because they're down there now tryin' to contract for his ship to commence haulin' our cattle.'

Murph nodded curtly. He wasn't the slightest bit interested. But Morgan was; he arose and followed Phil back out into the roadway.

Carl Peterson returned leading four saddled horses. He looped the reins at the tie-rack out front, came in, saw that the money had been moved, and raised his brows. One of his deputies pointed to one of the large lower drawers in Murph's desk. 'In there,' he murmured, and heaved himself up out of his chair with evident reluctance. 'You ready to load up and ride?'

Peterson nodded, looked around, then said, 'Sheriff; if you'd sort of lend a hand we'll get the sacks into our saddlebags and be on the way.'

Murph and the deputies went to work. The little sacks were not individually very heavy. But when a man had several in his arms, they began to feel not just heavy, but also very richly warm to embrace. One of the youthful deputies smiled and said if he had that much money he'd burn the candle at both ends until one or the other of them wore out. Another deputy said it wouldn't be the money that'd wear out.

There was no show of any particular interest when the five men made several trips in and out of the jailhouse. For one thing it was nearing noon and most of the pedestrian traffic was either eating or heading for some place where eating was going on. For another, the heat was higher than usual and that also drove folks indoors.

Murphy stood in the jailhouse doorway watching as the last few sacks were loaded. He shook his head slightly in quiet disapproval. Carl Peterson went methodically around checking all saddlebag buckles and flaps, then got astride, brushed his hatbrim to Murphy, turned and led out heading straight down towards the lower end of town

120

where the wide roadway pinched down a little, then swerved southward.

He was still standing there speculating on the chances of those four men getting all the way to San Francisco with that fortune in gold, when Morgan walked up with a man attired in the blue jacket and visored cap of a seaman. Morgan said, 'Sheriff; this here is Captain Blount. He's docked down the coast a ways near Mattole with his ship.'

Murph gravely shook Blount's hand. The seafaring man was short, very broad, and built like a beer-barrel. His hair was entirely grey and his face was sadly weather-checked. He looked to be a man in his mid-fifties. He said, 'I've been discussing taking several loads of cattle down to San Francisco or Stockton with some of your local cowmen, Sheriff. But that's not what brought me up here. I've been trying to explain to these other men that the talk of buried treasure in your area. . '

Murphy groaned out loud. Captain Blount looked startled. Morgan Forrest stood behind the sailor ready to burst into loud laughter. Blount said, 'What is it, Sheriff?'

'Cap'n,' exclaimed Murph. 'There is no buried treasure. There was, but it's gone.'

'Gone, Sheriff? How—gone?'

'Just plain gone, Cap'n. It belonged to the government, and the government sent for it and took it.'

'But that's not possible,' said Captain Bount. 'I was given to understand by the people who chartered my ship that—'

'Believe me, Cap'n Blount. That lousy ten thousand in gold is gone. And if you go up to Froman's camp to dig for it, you're likely to run into opposition. There could be other treasure-seekers up there. So far, I've had two run-ins with their kind. Now take my advice, Captain, and just go on back to your ship.'

'But what'll I tell the cavalry detail, Sheriff?'

Murph was stopped cold. 'Cavalry detail, Captain?'

'Yes; that's what I've been trying to tell this man and those other men down the road. I didn't come here to seek a cargo of cattle I came here to hunt buried treasure with a cavalry detail from Fort Shafter, down at San Francisco. The reason I was picked to bring the troopers northward was because I know these waters and also because I've had some luck at digging up other treasures.'

Morgan was no longer smiling even the slightest bit. Murph was stonily staring at the sailor. 'Where is this cavalry detail now?' he asked.

'It'll be along; probably arrive in the morning. There were six seasick horses. The captain said he'd have to walk his animals all the way and stop often to let the ill animals recoup.'

Murphy looked over Blount's head at Morgan. Forrest puckered up his lips in a noiseless whistle. Then he said, 'Maybe neither outfit knew the other outfit was sending men.'

Blount, picking up the thoughts whirling around him between Murphy and Morgan, scowled. 'What other outfit? I have my orders from the U.S. Marshal himself. Those cavalrymen have their orders from the military commandant of the Northern Defence Area.'

Murph drew up off his jailhouse doorjamb. 'Captain; do you know the U.S. Marshal for California when you see him?'

'Well certainly I know him, Sheriff. I've been transporting prisoners across the bay to San Quentin Prison for him for five years. I also know most of his deputies, for that matter.'

'Did you ever meet a deputy marshal named Cal Peterson?'

Blount didn't even hesitate. 'No sir, I have not. Unless he's been assigned to the San Francisco office within the past two days, since I weighed anchor to sail up here, he doesn't work out of the San Francisco office either.'

Morgan said, 'I'll go get the horses. You better get Barker and those others again, Sheriff.' He turned and went legging it swiftly toward the liverybarn.

Murph didn't even close his office door, he simply bumped Captain Blount aside and went trotting up towards Barker's saloon.

Blount righted himself and looked after Sheriff Crail with an indignant and bewildered expression. Then he waggled his head back and forth and muttered to himself that of all the crazy people he'd met in forty years this town of Douglas had the craziest.

Phil Barker was drowsily talking with Cap and Paul Standish when Murph barged in. Phil stopped in mid-sentence, struck by the look of urgency on Crail's face as he came forward.

'The money is gone,' said Murphy. This only increased the looks of puzzlement turned towards him by Standish, Bozeman and Phil Barker. 'Morgan and I dug up Froman's cache night before last,' Murphy explained, forcing himself to be calm with the knowledge in his head that those four imitation deputy U.S. marshals were moving fast by now, getting away. 'We brought it back to town after dark, put it in the safe in the jailhouse floor, and an hour or so ago we handed it over to four deputy U.S. marshals who rode off with it.'

'All right,' soothed Cap Bozeman. 'What's wrong with that?'

'They weren't federal marshals, Cap. They were impostors,' said Murphy. 'Now come on; we've got to go after them and fast.'

'Whoa,' said Phil, leaning across his bar. 'How do you

123

know they were impostors?'

'That sea captain you were trying to talk into hauling your cattle—'

'Captain Blount from San Francisco,' said Phil. 'What about him?'

'He tried to tell you fellers; he didn't come here to haul cattle. He brought up a detachment of cavalrymen to escort the money to his ship, then back down to San Francisco. He told me he knew every deputy U.S. marshal down there, and none of them are named Carl Peterson, which was the name the deputy marshal gave me, and I turned the money over to him. Now damn it all quit askin' fool questions and come along. Morgan's lining up the horses at the liverybarn.'

Phil pulled off his apron, looked around at his astonished customers, selected one man and tossed the apron at him. 'It's all yours until I can get back,' he said grabbed his gun-belt and went bolting out of the saloon in the wake of Murphy Crail and the others.

Morgan had the liveryman working at top speed rigging out their animals. He hadn't quite finished when Murph came lumbering up, so they all nagged at him to work faster.

When they finally got their animals Captain Blount and a dozen other onlookers, who'd heard the whole story up in Barker's saloon, were down there watching them get astride.

They left Douglas City the same way the imitation federal officers had also left it, and Murphy's ears were red with chagrin at the neat way he'd been taken in. 'They even had a letter signed by the governor himself,' he yelled at Cap as they sped along. 'They even had identification papers that would've convinced the President of the United States.'

'All right,' called back Cap, standing in his stirrups. 'Everyone makes mistakes, Murph; it's no crime to be wrong once in a while.'

'Ten thousand dollars worth, Cap?'

'Well,' conceded the older man. 'That *is* quite a figure to be wrong with I'll admit.'

It was just one o'clock when they lost sight of Douglas City behind them.

Chapter Fifteen

The southward country led steadily towards some chalky bluffs, topped by telluric stone with perhaps eight inches of top-soil over it from which grew brush and grass, flowers and endless varieties of scrub growth, but no trees. Had the sea been able, it would have gnawed away those chalky cliffs, but miles west by another set of bluffs, lower, thicker, darker with the veins of congealed granite shot through them, which the sea had been beating against since the beginning of Time and hadn't more than rounded their corners. Until this darker wall fell, the chalky cliffs were secure. They were also ideal for riders to use in studying the onward land, southward, because it sloped away for many miles before trees appeared, the road across it greyly, dustily visible.

But there was also a glare, which normally there wasn't. This was neither arid nor hot country. Ordinarily there'd be a hazy blur to distances, part fog, part perpetual mist. Today there was no such ally and as the riders slowed to look, the glare blinded them.

'If they didn't take the coast road,' said Cap Bozeman who'd just come up the coast road a few days before, 'then they had to cut inland towards the forest. Them's the only two directions for 'em. They sure didn't go back towards town or we'd have seen them, and if they'd gone west they'd be swimmin' by now.'

Morgan said, 'One man come with me and we'll scout the north country. It's not likely they went that way, but we'll scout it while the rest of you head right on down the road, which is about where they'll be—ridin' along and laughin' fit to bust.'

Phil Barker looked at Murph, who nodded, so Phil went with Morgan Forrest, jogging northward. Murph led the others on down the road, alternately loping and going at a fast walk.

What bothered Murph, the farther they rode without seeing anyone ahead, was the possibility, after nightfall forced he and his possemen to halt, of the thieves going right on down the road.

Cap angled away heading towards a low promontory on the inland side of the broad roadway. He rode up it, sat a while, then rode down it and caught up with Murphy. 'Dust cloud about three, four miles ahead,' he reported. 'Too far for me to say it was riders, but it's sure coming up this way—whatever it is.'

There was considerable traffic of one variety or another on the coast road. Tracks were thick and endless. Murph read sign as he went along but only to kill time, not because he was hopeful at all. Cap muttered disgustedly that at any other time they'd have passed at least one emigrant wagon or spring-buggy, or horseman, by now, who could've told them whether or not four men riding in a group were on ahead.

That eventually happened when the dust cloud Cap had seen came boiling across some dunes, dipped and rose through a series of wind-scoured chalk knobs and got close enough for them to hail it.

The conveyance was a coach, privately chartered, going on up the coast from the town of Mattole with a fishing party. The driver had a lively hitch; even after coming so far his animals were still full of vinegar and had to be fought down to a halt beginning back a quarter mile from where he saw Murph and Cap signalling him. He might not have fully stopped even then, though, but where sunlight struck the horsemen, he saw the glint of Murph's badge.

The sheriff asked where the coach was bound, got his

answer and asked where it had come from. When the whip said, 'Mattole,' Murph asked if he'd seen four horsemen riding together. The whip had. 'About four miles on down where the cedars begin, Sheriff, was where we passed 'em. They waved an' we waved back. They was riding with looped reins eating as they went, but they weren't goin' fast.'

'You're sure there were four?'

'You bet I'm sure, Sheriff; there was three younger fellers and an older feller.'

That was undoubtedly the gang. Murph waved the coach on and saluted the driver with an upflung arm, then he and Cap pushed ahead for a mile in a long lope before settling back again to an easier, slower gait.

'Not expecting anything yet,' mused Murph. 'Peterson really made a fool out of me.'

Cap said nothing but every now and then he'd turn to look anxiously back behind them, and northward. He was obviously concerned with the whereabouts of Morgan Forrest and Phil Barker. Murph told him to forget it; that Barker and Forrest would show up sooner or later.

'It's the later I'm worryin' about,' stated Cap. 'Very much later an' we're likely to run onto those four outlaws, in which case we're going to need Phil and Morgan Forrest right quick.'

The shadows began to come, just a hint at first because the sea lay out there catching all light and throwing it back towards the land perpetuating a long afternoon into an awfully long evening. Those were pastel shadows without a showing of the hard, blood-red splashes a lowering sun showed elsewhere. Nor were there any quick, sooty shadows in the little arroyos or down across the face of those chalky barrancas. Only soft-settling waves of opaque colour dropping layer upon layer.

The heat lingered and Murph commented about the lateness, about the distance they'd come since leaving

128

Douglas, and also about the distance they'd traversed since splitting off from Morgan and Phil.

'If they're following a trail it'll be the wrong one,' he said. 'They'll be headin' north towards the mountains and we'll be heading due south towards Mattole.'

Cap had no comment. He'd already expressed his anxiety over being divided like this. But they simultaneously picked up the flash and spark of dying sunlight reflecting off metal somewhere ahead and forgot their other worries to concentrate on this interesting phenomenon; either someone was coming up the road towards them, or someone was hiding at the side of the road waiting for them.

'They'd be expecting pursuit,' mused Murphy. 'I doubt if they'd be expecting it this soon, but they'd be wary all the same.'

Cap concurred, watching that spot in the cedars down there where the light had flashed a time or two then had died. 'They'd know you a half mile off by your size, Murph, but I could get closer and scout them up a little.'

'Get shot,' grunted Murph. 'That's what you'd get, Cap.' He jutted his chin. 'We'll leave the road a ways ahead and try swinging around behind them.'

But they never did that. Cap saw two more of those quick, sharp flashes and raised in his stirrups like an old dog on a new trail. 'Soldiers,' he exclaimed. 'Those are reflections off sabre scabbards or I'm not a foot high. I should've know that, confound it, I've seen it enough times. There's some cavalry down there in those cedar trees, makin' camp.'

Cap was correct. Murph stayed on the road until they were well within musket-range, and didn't stop until they saw the hobbled horses with their 'U.S.' brand. By then they also saw the horseguard and he, who had evidently been watching their approach for some time, waved them on in. They threw the trooper a wave and passed straight on down to where the balance of that detachment was lolling in cedar-shade looking tired but not particularly trail-worn.

Their officer commanding was a captain from San Francisco who said his name was Gerald Hunt. He was a sinewy, ramrod-straight man in his late twenties with the wholesome, sun-bronzed features of a seasoned officer. He invited Cap and Sheriff Crail to have a drink of coffee with him before supper, and Murph waited until the officer had spoken first, about what he was doing in this part of the country, before Murph dropped his bombshell.

'That money is gone, Captain,' he said, afterwards. 'Every golden dollar of it.'

Not only the captain, but his sergeant-major, a grizzled, squat, reddish-haired and reddish-faced man, was also shocked into jumping to their feet. The enlisted dragoons, making enough talk of their own over where a small fire was being coaxed to life, evidently didn't hear that statement.

Murph then proceeded to explain what had happened, how and when it had happened. The captain and his subordinate listened with close attention to the very last, then the sergeant-major said, 'Well now, Captain; it'd be them same devils we passed a while back. Four of 'em, you say, Sheriff: Three younger ones an' the older one?'

Murph nodded. 'How far back did you see them?' he asked.

'Not far,' responded the sergeant-major, and turned. 'We could overtake 'em, Captain. Leave all but a squad, take the strongest horses . . .' He waited.

Captain Hunt nodded. 'Pick the men,' he told his subordinate. 'Have horses saddled for you and me, Sergeant. If the light holds we can do it, I believe.' Hunt

130

turned to Murph and Cap Bozeman. 'Those other two
men you said split off from you to scout northward,
Sheriff; will they return to the road and come southward?'

Murph didn't know and said so. He'd expected some
sign of Forrest and Barker long before this, unless they
were paralleling the road somewhere off to the north, as
he said to the officer; possibly doing that to make certain
the four outlaws didn't turn inland and make for the
mountains where they would almost certainly escape.

Captain Hunt had a dry observation to make on that
'The difficulty,' he said, 'is that with an army unit you
control all details sent out. With civilians it's a
haphazard, hit-or-miss matter, about like this one. You
don't know where your men are.'

Cap Bozeman spoke up, setting aside his emptied tin
cup. 'Captain; the difficulty isn't lack of control—the
difficulty is how long it takes soldiers to get moving.
Every second we're here is one more second that ten
thousand in gold is getting farther off.'

Hunt took his mild rebuke with good humour, turned
and bawled for the sergeant-major to hasten. They got
astride, Captain Hunt, his dog-robber, and four troopers,
plus Murph and Cap Bozeman. Their horses had been
used almost enough for one day so they favoured them
remarking to one another that this also applied to the
horses of the outlaws.

They had to travel a good mile before breaking
through the cedars where the road abruptly swung
westerly out towards a gigantic stone promontory which
jutted farther away, out into the sea. But Cap Bozeman
was in the lead and kept straight, letting the road move
away from them while Cap found a little cow-trail which
went arrow-straight, and in this fashion lopped off almost
a half-hour's riding.

The sun was dropping away very steadily now, turning

a greeny shade of ancient copper, with thin little fleecy clouds continually passing across its coarse face. The heat was gone too; salt-scent was all around, carried inland by one of those breezes that eternally ran as far as the northward hills and there were shredded by the forests.

Murph was beginning to regain his confidence. He said he felt certain the outlaws would hole up before dark, even if they knew the trails ahead because they had to favour their animals. It was a good guess; men whose continued freedom—perhaps even their lives—depended upon four saddle animals, weren't very likely to abuse the beasts.

They came onto the coast road again and from the rear of their file a soldier sang out to his sergeant-major that they had a pair of riders coming down towards them from behind and to their left.

The line halted in shade down where the cedars began again, and where the road, consisting of some endless number of tiny prehistoric shells had been ground to a dusty silver-white colour. Murph and Cap Bozeman dismounted to rest the backs of their horses, watched those two oncoming riders and recognized them before they were within shooting range.

'Barker and Forrest,' said Murph to the captain. 'It looks like they've been paralleling us.'

Phil and Morgan slowed to a kidding-jarring trot and came on up into the cedar trees like that. Murph introduced them around, then got back into the saddle and motioned for Cap to lead off again.

Phil said he and Morgan had looked for sign over along the foothills and had found none. Then they'd spotted the line of riders taking that short-cut back where the road swung out towards the sea, and had decided to come on down and have a look.

In his turn, Murph explained about the military

132

presence and Morgan said that he was sure, if they kept this up, they would overtake the bandits. For a while longer they all rode in solemn silence, then Phil took Cap and loped on down through the trees seeking an opening which would permit them to see far ahead.

The sergeant-major made some low comment to his captain about missing supper. The captain's reply was short and indistinguishable to the others. Those four troopers strung out in pairs towards the end of their little column were wiry, tough men accustomed to missing meals and to hard rides. They came along with that quiet *élan* of seasoned campaigners, watchful, ready, impervious to most personal discomforts, one never found in recruits.

Phil and Cap Bozeman appeared suddenly out of the westerly trees and halted facing back in the centre of the road. They had something to report. Murph reached them first, then the dragoons also came on up and stopped.

'There's a ranch ahead,' said Phil. 'They got their supper-fire going; you can see smoke coming from the chimney. If the thieves changed horses or rested, that'd likely be the place.'

Bozeman let Phil finish then said, 'There's a stage-station a few miles farther along where I stopped on my way back from Mattole a few nights back. If they didn't stop at the ranch chances are they stopped at the coach-stop.' Then Cap said quietly, 'But there's no visible sign of 'em at all.'

'Head for the ranch first,' stated Murph, while Captain Hunt gravely concurred by nodding his head. At once they all moved out again, through increasing layers of dusky shadows. It was lighter beyond the trees, while in among them it seemed already to be close to nightfall.

Chapter Sixteen

They jogged out of the trees, which were short, fat, dowdy Coast Cedars, headed for the ranch which lay in a long cover with most of the buildings facing away from the sea where raw winds would come, and had the sun at their backs as the road turned so as to pass squarely through the large ranchyard. But there was no longer much warmth to that sun.

A man stepped from a cook-shack to fling away wash-water, and saw their party approaching. At first he only shot them one glance, then, evidently spotting the armed soldiers in blue, he turned slowly to put a long, hard look forward.

Captain Hunt said, 'We by-passed this place earlier in the day. That man down there acts as though the sight of troopers is rare.'

'It is,' stated Phil Barker. 'Between the forts down around San Francisco and some little log outposts on up into Oregon, there's been no reason to have soldiers hangin' around for the past few years.'

The man down there with his porcelain wash-bowl, set the thing on a bench at the back of the little shack and walked around front towards the roadway. There, he came to a sagging old wooden gate with green and red lichen on the wood, and quietly waited.

Murph edged over to be nearest the man when they came dustily into the ranchyard. He said, 'We're looking for four horsemen who passed by here a short while back. Three younger men and an older one.'

The man, dressed in rudely patched work clothing, was

134

evidently a hired hand. He was chewing tobacco with an unconsciously measured rhythm. He didn't answer until he'd made a slow examination of every man, then he said, 'Wall; 'bout hour back four fellers went through. They didn't stop though; just tossed me a wave an' moseyed on. I couldn't say whether they was young, old, or in-between, Sheriff. I warn't close enough to make 'em out too good.'

Captain Hunt said, 'Are the owners of this place at home?'

The countryman waggled his head. 'Down t'the city. Ever' y'ar they go down t'the city for a couple weeks, after the work's done, y'see.'

Hunt said, 'Thanks,' and motioned for Murph to move out. As the little cavalcade passed on through the man still leaned back there on his gate chewing his cud and studying them with the fatalistic phlegmaticism one so often encountered in men shackled to the soil from the sun-up of their lives to the sundown of it, doing the same things over and over and over.

No one said anything but the impression that country-man had left with them was the same. One thing was plain enough; he hadn't lied. Even if he was capable of direct misrepresentation he couldn't have hid the fact that he was lying from them.

Cap Bozeman went ahead a little distance as though to reassure himself he hadn't been wrong about that coach-stop on a few miles. When the others came up, Cap was standing beside his horse off to the side of the road where several great shaggy old blue-gum trees stood making the area redolent with their antiseptic odour.

Ahead, with shadows mottling it in among the eucalyptus trees, stood a stone-walled, low-roofed build-ing which looked more fort than stage-stop. Even its small windows were set high in each wall, and had steel bars in front of them.

'Used to be a fort,' said the sergeant-major. 'I never been in it, but I've heard talk among the oldtimers. Folks used to head for that place when the Diggers got on the rampage.'

Diggers meant Coast Range Indians; a very low, primitive fish-and-grub-eating variety of savages, never very numerous but always worth watching because of their inherent facility for treachery. The others listened but weren't interested particularly, so Cap got back astride and led the way on down towards it.

There was a huge corral out back which had been divided into separate corrals simply by making dividing fences. The thing was clearly designed to resemble the wheel of a wagon; each corral narrowed down near the place where the hub would have been, and there, serving all the corrals, was a circular, stone watering trough.

The corralled animals looked up with horsy interest as soon as the riders passed out into plain sight bound towards the front of the building. Several of them neighed, and this brought two men to the front door. Both were roughly dressed, flat-bellied labourers of some kind. One had a shaggy set of whiskers while the other one, taller and shock-headed, was not just clean-shaven, but also much younger than the bearded man.

This time, though, the strangers they saw studying them made no move to walk out front. They seemed content to stand in the doorway staring. Murph, who was up front with Cap Bozeman, saw the shorter, thicker man turn his furry face and speak shortly to the younger man. At once this latter individual stepped back inside.

Phil Barker, directly behind Murph, said, 'I detect an odd smell, Sheriff. A right odd smell.' Actually, there was no odour other than the peculiar astringent scent of those eucalyptus trees; what Phil meant was that he had a

136

premonition about this place and those two men down there.

Captain Hunt leaned and spoke to the sergeant-major who turned, jerked his head at two of the troopers and cut off from the others swinging towards the rear of the building. That barrel-shaped bearded man saw this and turned to call something to his companion who was inside the building. Then the bearded one walked out and stopped some twenty feet from the door, waiting.

Murph and Cap stopped to study the bearded man. The others came up around them and also halted. For a while no one spoke but eventually the bearded man lifted heavy lips in a mirthless smile and boomed out a greeting.

'Climb down an' water your stock,' he said. 'Night'll be along directly. We got plenty places you can camp.'

Captain Hunt ignored this invitation. 'We're looking for three young men riding with an older man. They went past here not very long ago, I think.'

The way-station man puckered up his forehead and squinted. 'If they did, Cap'n, we sure never saw 'em. But then we was probably out back doin' the chores. Or maybe inside fixin' supper.'

Murph and Phil Barker exchanged a look. The road in both directions was unobstructed. Even if those way-station men had been out back, as this one suggested, they still would have seen movement in either direction on the road exactly as they'd just picked up the movement of the present riders sitting in front of them.

Murph said, 'Mister; they're wanted men. Not just by local lawmen, but also by the federal government.' It was mildly said, and yet unmistakably was a warning. The bearded man, however, shook his head at Murphy.

'Lots of time riders get by 'thout us seeing them, Sheriff. We got no call to have any truck with 'em anyway, unless of course they got to stop for water or to camp nearby.'

The sergeant-major and his two companions came riding down the side of the rock building looking stern. They passed right by the bearded man and halted facing Gerald Hunt. In a voice loud enough for the bearded man to hear, the sergeant-major said, 'Sir; there were four tucked-up horses in a corral back there with the saddle-sweat still fresh on their backs.'

This brought the shock-headed, tall, rawboned man out of the way-station. He was wearing a gun around his middle which he hadn't been wearing before. He walked up beside the bearded man, his face troubled but tough-set. He seemed to feel both he and his partner were in trouble, but he didn't seem the least likely to concede that nor to turn humble in the face of it.

Way-station men weren't hired to live in the perilous existence required of them in vulnerable, lonely places, unless they were tough and resourceful. They were also supposed to be honest, but that wasn't a prerequisite, only a hope, of their employers.

Captain Hunt looked coolly at those two, stepped down and gave the order for his subordinate to also dismount the other troopers. Murph, Cap and Barker also stepped off. Morgan Forrest did an odd thing; he dismounted on the right-hand, or incorrect, side of his mount which put the beast between his body and the way-station attendants. Everyone who saw this knew what it meant: Forrest sensed trouble coming.

'Now wait a minute,' protested the bearded man, holding forth both hands, palms outward. 'Sure we got horses with saddle-stains on 'em. We rode out this morning lookin' for strays in the hills, then we come back this afternoon, got fresh critters an' went back.'

The sergeant-major's scarred, pugnacious face lifted a

little. 'Mister; you're lyin',' he said, the flap of his holster neatly tucked under and his right hand resting upon the exposed gun-butt. 'If you'd done that, them horses around there which you'd rode this mornin', wouldn't still have wet sweat on their backs, would they?'

It had been, apparently, a spontaneous effort on the attendant's part, and it had palpably failed. He dropped his arms and stoically watched the captain start walking towards the rear of the building. His taller, rougher-looking companion was trying to watch Morgan and Murph, Phil and Cap Bozeman. He showed stubbornness but he also showed desperation. The odds were too great, if trouble started, and he was too far from the door at his back to make it back into the stone fort.

Murph, looking straight at the bearded man, said, 'Mister; don't make it any worse. How much did they pay for the fresh horses?'

'Who?' asked the attendant, and when Murph didn't answer, when the men facing him turned hard and bitter towards him, he let out a big breath and shook his head. 'The trouble with lawmen an' soljers, Sheriff, is that they just don't have no belief in folks.'

'Not lying ones, anyway,' replied Murph dryly. 'Come on; spit it out. Stalling isn't going to help them a whole lot and it isn't going to help you at all.'

The younger man loosened his shoulders, looked down at his companion, and seemed to believe they had no alternative but to tell the truth. His friend rolled up his eyes. At that moment Captain Hunt came picking his way through the weeds alongside the house, halted, drew his service-revolver and said from forty feet back, 'Disarm them, Sergeant.' Then he also said, 'There's a cocked gun pointed at your backs, men. If you want to make a fight of it, the one with the gun dies first.'

Hunt's troopers reached for their guns too. Those two

way-station men moved just their eyes. The younger one hadn't said a word up to now, but with the breath running shallow in him now, he whispered something to his companion which the bearded man seemed to heed.

'No need for all this, boys,' he said a trifle squeakily. 'Cap'n; you can come from behind us.' While he was speaking the sergeant-major disarmed the tall one and moved off to one side also covering the pair with the young man's own gun.

Captain Hunt put up his revolver, walked slowly on up, turned when he was nearby and said to the bearded man. 'How long ago did they leave? Mister; if you lie to me one more time you're going back to San Francisco in chains. Now—how long ago?'

'Less'n an hour, Cap'n, and if we hadn't sold 'em the horses they'd have shot us sure. They were a mean bunch, tucked up and travel-worn. Meaner'n a snake, Cap'n.'

Phil snorted disdainfully. Morgan moved out around his horse into plain view. Until he did that none of the others had known he had a forty-five in his right fist. He leathered the weapon. Murph stonily regarded those two. 'How much did they pay you?' he asked, and the answer came right back.

'Forty dollars each for them critters, Sheriff. But you got to appreciate they were fine animals; no twenty-dollar crowbaits at all. Good, big strong animals, Sheriff.'

'They were so mean,' murmured Cap Bozeman, 'an' you were so scairt that they actually paid you top price. Why; so's you'd delay any pursuit or maybe set us off on a wrong trail?'

'Well,' muttered the bearded man. 'They did want us to do somethin' like that. But Ralph an' me—we told 'em we was upstandin' men and wouldn't do nothing which warn't—'

'Get their names,' barked Captain Hunt, heading in obvious disgust towards his horse. The sergeant-major moved in at once to comply.

Murph also walked over, but he didn't say a thing, he simply held out his left hand, palm up. The bearded man looked down, then up. He started to protest. Murph jabbed him in the stomach with that outstretched hand. He towered over them both and was almost as thick as they were combined. The bearded man muttered a painful curse, dug into his pocket and brought out a number of shiny gold coins. He looked sadly at them, then dropped each coin singly and very reluctantly into Murphy's hand. Murph took the money over and handed it to Captain Hunt, still without speaking. Then he went over to his grey and stepped across leather. He wasn't as mad as he was contemptuous. He'd have respected them more even if they'd made a fight of it.

'Where are they going to camp?' he asked.

The younger man looked up. 'If you don't get 'em,' he said, 'and they figure out we told you, Sheriff, our hides won't be worth a damn in this part of the country ever again.'

'They're not worth a damn right now,' retorted Murphy. 'If the army doesn't get you fired, I'll be back in a few days to see if you're still here. If you are, you're goin' up to Douglas City to jail. Now; where are they going to make camp for the night?'

The bearded man lifted a limp arm pointing southward. 'There's a cove about three miles onward. By the time you fellers get there it'll be close to dark. There's an old cow-camp shack down there with a well behind it. We told 'em of that place.' He dropped his arm disconsolately. 'That's where they figure to hole up tonight.'

'One more thing,' said Murphy. 'If either one of you leaves this shack before tomorrow morning, and we see you, you're going to be shot on sight. That is a promise.'

Captain Hunt ordered his men to mount up. They did, and the cavalcade headed on down the road. Behind them stood two very troubled way-station attendants. Also behind them but much farther away, the sun was teetering upon a high peak.

Chapter Seventeen

After the stage-station, a series of serrated high bluffs appeared on their left, back where the higher country began. These cliffs marched westerly as though to force a juncture with the sea itself, although they never quite accomplished that, for the strip of land between them and the distant sea remained obdurately flat, or more or less so, all the way down to the San Francisco Bay area. But after the stage-station they encountered no more ranches nor other signs of permanent human habitation. But the road seemed to get better, indicating there would be a town somewhere down through this country.

There was a town but it was still a long way off. The town of Mattole. It lay in a coastal valley of considerable size where those serrated cliffs abruptly bent inland and retreated several miles, leaving a land-locked, thoroughly protected broad little valley which was suitable for just about anything they wished to grow down there because in all the recorded history of Mattole there had never been even one day of frost.

But between Mattole and up where Murphy Crail and the others were heading into the broken country, were a series of little rough arroyos, neither very deep nor very long, running from north to south or roughly from the serrated cliffs to the sea, but they were broad, and nearly all of them, lying one after the other straight down towards Mattole, had trees in them, and underbrush.

It was as though the bulging cliffs to the northward had puckered the coastal strip of flat land, buckling it, forcing it to adopt a pleated effect. Then too, with the equable climate, whatever seed birds dropped there over the years, had evidently taken root and flourished. The first of these places Murph's party came to had those dowdy cedar trees, some sage, some chapparal, and a variety of sea-grape that served no purpose under the sun except to hold the land in place. Cap Bozeman and the soldiers had used the stretch of road not too long before. Cap told Murphy Crail if they were doggoned careful they wouldn't make any noise. Gerald Hunt called a halt when they were nearing that place and asked if anyone knew whether or not there was water in that secluded place. Cap Bozeman said there was not; he also said the gulch those way-station attendants had meant was on a couple more miles; they'd know it by the old rough-plank shack down there.

Hunt said he thought they should now await full darkness and no one argued with that. They proceeded another half mile or so, then turned off into a blue-gum patch, dismounted and loosened cinchas all around. Captain Hunt detailed one of his men to watch their animals, which hungrily went around dragging reins and seeking something to eat besides sea-grape and sage.

Murph took Phil Barker and scouted southward. Keeping hidden was no problem; there was more than ample cover on all sides. The ensuing broad little pleat in the hills was about like the one where they'd dismounted, but farther along, still visible in the twilight, was a tall eucalyptus stand looking as though it had been deliberately planned to form a windbreak. They crept ahead, meaning to see if this wasn't the place where the old cow-camp was, then Phil caught Murph's arm and halted him. There was a definite smell of cooking food in the dusk.

'Satisfied?' Phil asked.

Murph nodded. He was satisfied. 'It's been a long trail,' he muttered. 'I'm kind of ashamed of myself for pushing the grey horse so far without a decent rest.'

'He'll get plenty of rest from now on,' said Phil, looking ahead. 'Why do you suppose when we can smell the smoke we can't see the fire?'

'That shack must be the other side of the windbreak. They'll have their fire inside there. Maybe in a stove or a fireplace.'

Phil accepted that. 'Want to get any closer?' he asked.

Murph nodded, so they started ahead. Actually, between the undergrowth and the darkening night they had only to be careful of the noise they made; no one could have detected their movement anyway; between the shaggy old blue-gum trees, the uneven and irregular brush, and that peek-a-boo moon rising now to roll in and out among the misty high clouds, they were safe from any kind of detection except direct frontal confrontation.

Phil was careful though, moving with the gliding gait of a prowling redskin. He was good at it. When they got close enough to detect flickering light from beyond the eucalyptus windbreak through a square-hewn window, he stopped and hunkered. Murph did the same.

Phil said, 'If we get closer someone's liable to be out there watchin'.' Murph nodded. In his opinion the important thing was not to arouse the outlaws at all, until they had their full force up this close; the important thing was to make sure they'd finally reached the end of their particular trail. They had.

Phil turned back. Murph let him lead all the way, but when Captain Hunt loomed up in the night, Murph went directly to him with an idea.

'Captain; the shack is on the south side of a blue-gum grove. There's a light inside. We figure from that they're probably eating or bedding down. Anyway; I think they're being inside is going to make all the difference in the world for us.'

'Yes,' concurred the captain. 'We'll surround them and—'

'Captain,' said Murph. 'Surrounding them isn't what's got to be done. You'll see when you get down there. We've got to split up. You take your men and sneak down the road southward on foot. It's dark enough to make it if you don't make a sound. Then you block that southward roadway while I stay up on this end of the road. They can't escape inland; those saw-toothed cliffs back there couldn't be climbed by the most experienced climbers in the country. And straight ahead is the ocean.'

Hunt listened and nodded his head. 'On foot?' he asked.

Murph nodded. 'We'll keep your horses up with ours and leave them all about where they are now so neither band of 'em'll smell the others and nicker.'

Again Hunt bobbed his head up and down. 'Bottle them up,' he murmured, referring to the unsuspecting outlaws in that shack down there, 'and cut them off. Very good, Sheriff Crail, very good. Now suppose you show us how to get down there into position.'

Hunt called his sergeant-major, ordered the men all forward with carbines, to leave their horses with the civilians from Douglas City, then struck out with Murph and Phil Barker.

It was easier the second time. Phil used the same approach to show Captain Hunt and his men the orange glow through that tree-shadowed window before he struck out on a tangent, taking them over to the road, across it, and into the brush on the ocean-side. There, Murph drew his sixgun and waited, covering the house. This would be the most crucial phase for the men inside the house as well as outside it; if noise was made the outlaws were going to know they'd been tracked down.

Murph sat and sweated while Barker and the troopers

went gliding straight southward. The moon popped from behind some filmy clouds. Light came instantly, eerie, cold and hauntingly beautiful. Those rearward majestic cliffs, proudly perpendicular, glowed with cotton softness. Somewhere off on Murph's right the sea sullenly boomed against a granite shore.

Phil came back slightly breathless. The lower half of the trap, he said, was set. Now they moved back a yard at a time being more careful than ever, to where the others waited in motionless anxiety.

'Damn,' breathed Cap Bozeman. 'I thought sure they's snuck up an' grabbed you. What took so long?'

Murph didn't answer and Phil went over to check the tied horses and fetch back two carbines, his own and Murphy's weapon. The plan was simple as Murph explained it. They would sneak down as close to the cow-camp shack as it was prudent to get, bearing in mind those were armed and desperate men in there, then they'd fan out across the roadway. Finally, said Murphy, he'd call out. They might surrender without a scrap when he told them how they were bottled up.

'Not in a hundred years,' disagreed Morgan Forrest. 'They've got ten thousand in gold in there with them. Outside, with us, all they've got is a bleak future of maybe ten years in a federal prison. That kind of a choice doesn't leave men much to decide. I'd fight and so would the rest of you.'

Murph shrugged. He didn't believe they'd surrender either, but he hoped they would. The others had their carbines and were ready. Murph turned and started back down towards the blue-gum windbreak for the last time.

Phil Barker had Cap Bozeman following him. Morgan Forrest went with Murphy Crail. They'd made this trip without mishap enough times, considering its relatively short distance, for the two leaders to encounter no difficulty. When they were down where that light shone, they halted. Phil said they must've had candles in their saddlebags. Murph wasn't interested either way, whether they'd brought the light with them or whether they'd found it in the shack—but he thought the latter more probable than the former. Not many men carried candles.

When they were close enough to pick up the scent of fragrant tobacco smoke, Murph pointed, urging Phil to get over closer to the road, Barker obeyed with a wolfish grin. He was enjoying himself.

Where the road passed straight southward, Bozeman and Forrest could see the little tumble-down shack in the soft-sad moonlight. It stood back from the roadway about three hundred feet, and blended with its unkempt surroundings. The blue-gum trees were tall, old, and as shaggy as they always were, casting tall shadows across the bleached-bone roof of the building. To Murph and the others, if those outlaws ran out, their only safety lay in staying back in the shadows of that shack and those scruffy tall trees. Then, because of the poor light back there, they'd be hard to see.

Phil took Cap and crossed the roadway. Then they divided, Cap remaining closer to the roadway, Phil fanning out on over several hundred feet into a flourishing, coarse stand of sea-grape.

Murph and Morgan Forrest stayed on the near side of the road with the shack well in sight. They were less than a hundred feet apart. Murph gazed southward where moonlight traced out the coast highway. It ran arrow-straight for about a mile; well beyond the underbrush over where Captain Hunt and his troopers were, but after that the uneven escarpment of land southward forced it to hump up, drop down out of sight in the next pleat of land, then heave itself upwards again, bending out towards the sea and back again, as crooked as a huge old mottled snake.

Murph put down his carbine, drew in a breath and sang out. His words broke the silence with a startling, harsh echo. 'Peterson; this is Sheriff Crail from Douglas City. You're cut off by soldiers and possemen.'

Murph said no more for a moment. Inside the shack, that light instantly went out. Otherwise there was no sound, no hint of movement. Murph called out again.

'You can have it any way you want it, but it's going to keep someone from getting killed if you leave your guns in there and march out—all four of you.'

This time there was a sound as someone evidently struck at a wooden obstruction to see better. There were two little stingy windows in front and a square, elongated hole where the door had once been. There was a window on the north wall, too; that's the one they first had spotted the light through. Murph had no idea if there were windows out back or on the south wall, but he thought there would be.

Morgan, watching the house intently, shook his head. 'That was a waste of breath,' he stated.

But no gunshots erupted. The silence ran on, changed now, however, no longer drowsily quiet and peaceful. There was a menacing quality to it which kept the men from Douglas City sharply alert and watchful.

'They're talkin' it over,' hazarded Morgan. 'They'll probably think that talk of soldiers is a lie. But it's a darned wonder when they were running southward and Hunt's detail was riding northward, they didn't see each other.'

Murph said, 'Those little freakish things happen. What I'm hoping is that they'll think I've got a big enough posse to whip them anyway, whether they believe there are troopers around or not.'

Still though, the silence ran on. Murph squirmed, speculating that they might be sneaking out the back windows of the shack. He called out again.

'Peterson—or whatever your name is—make it easy on yourself. There's no place you can run to.'

This time, Murphy got an answer. Someone in there slanted a shot through the doorway in the direction of Murphy's voice. It was close but not close enough. Instantly, Morgan drove an answering bullet through the doorway at the flash of red flame in there. Then silence again until the recognizable voice of the man calling himself Carl Peterson sang out.

'Sheriff: how many men out there with you?'

'Enough,' Murph answered.

'Sheriff; make it worth their while for the ride and the inconvenience. I'll bring out a thousand dollars and put it where you can see it. Then I'll go back inside and you can come get it. Divvy it up; it ought to pay your men real good. All you got to do then is ride off.'

Murph was guessing about where Peterson was, behind those flimsy walls. He cocked his carbine and raised it. That old shack was too punky to turn a bullet. Those men inside had only one advantage—they weren't visible—but otherwise those walls weren't going to be much help if enough lead was pumped into the building.

'Sheriff,' sang out Peterson again. 'All right; we'll make it *two* thousand. Now there's plenty of gold for everyone. What say, Sheriff?'

Murph fired straight at the wall where he figured Peterson was. This time, Cap Bozeman and Phil Barker also let fly at the house, but Captain Hunt and his concealed troopers southward didn't fire even one round. Murph thought he knew what Hunt was doing; waiting, leading the outlaws to believe they only had those four men from Douglas City aligned against them. Hunt was

150

purposefully baiting the outlaws into making a southward dash for freedom.

Peterson's furious voice roared curses above the
return-fire his men threw out the doorway and the
glassless windows. Evidently Murph had come close
enough to startle him, and to also enrage him, with that
bullet.

Chapter Eighteen

For several minutes the fight raged, then Murph and Morgan Forrest eased off to reload. Cap and Phil took this as a cue to also stop firing and did so.

Now that ghostly silence came down again, frightening and all-encompassing. Overhead, the moon soared closer to the serrated cliffs. Within another couple of hours it would be far down behind those ramparts somewhere. Then the broad savannah where the battle was going on would be steeped in leaden gloom.

From southward an owl hooted thrice in swift succession the way horned owls invariably hooted. It was such a perfect imitation Morgan and Murph were doubtful that it was an imitation at first.

'No owls around after this gunfire,' mused Murph. 'That'll be Hunt letting us know he's waiting down there.'

Morgan was wry about that. 'Be better if he'd let us know he'd figured out a way to blast those men out of that cussed shack.'

A shot from the northward window drove lead into one of the blue-gums not far from where Morgan was crouching. He dropped flat with a whistling curse and twisted to reply, but the gunman had danced backwards the moment he'd let fly, so there was nothing to aim at. Morgan removed his hat, put it on the ground at his side, took a long rest on both elbows and waited.

Cap and Phil opened up again. They'd wiggled around until they could fire directly through the front windows and doorway. They tried raking the inside although they couldn't angle their bullets too well, positioned as they were. One thing they could and did do, though, was dump twelve bullets from their Winchester carbines through the windows and doorway about as fast as they could lever up and tug-off. That thunderous, continual rattle and roar drowned out every other sound, even the answering guns from inside the shack. But those stopped eventually and the Winchesters kept right on spraying lead until each man had emptied his weapon. Then the silence returned, but now it had an acid scent to it from burnt gunpowder.

For ten seconds there wasn't a shot. Morgan broke that lull by firing towards the window at a shadow. The shadow dropped away and Morgan grunted to himself, not certain he'd scored a hit but believing it was very probably that he had.

That ended it. There wasn't another shot fired for a very long while. Murph got anxious about that silence. He told Morgan that Peterson had made all his judgements by now; he'd probably decided the possemen from Douglas City were only four in number and were hiding in the gloom and undergrowth north of their hideout.

'Which means we'd better try creeping towards the back,' said Morgan. 'That's where they'll try to slip out and make their run for it. Their animals are out there somewhere.'

Murph procrastinated. If he and Morgan remained in place there'd be no hole in their line. But also, if they stayed and the outlaws made their rush, it was possible they might catch Hunt's soldiers off-guard and go right through them. He said, 'Morgan; stay here. I'll be back in a minute.'

'If at all,' muttered Forrest, and eased up slightly to see what Murph was up to.

He crawled with some difficulty through the rank growth, reached the blue-gums where nothing grew, not even grass, and crept fast until he was near the far corner of the shack. There, he dropped down, rolled to get a brace of big old trees between his body and the shack, then peered around back.

There were two windows back there as he'd surmised but there was also another of those doorless openings which had been for a rear exit, and he hadn't thought that probable at all. As he watched, a man with a carbine leaned through looking left and right, testing the night before he ran out. Murph raised his carbine with no thought in mind of hitting that razor-thin silhouette, and fired across the back of the house. It hadn't been his intention to hit the house either. His bullet struck a southward tree with solid force. That would warn Captain Hunt and his men the outlaws were moving towards the rear of the shack.

That man in the doorway tumbled backwards so suddenly Murph heard him slam into someone else in there, and both of them heartily swore. Murph dumped another slug into the southward trees and brush, then turned and began snaking his way back where Morgan had finally comprehended what all that had been about. Morgan was grinning when Murph came, breathing loudly. Neither of them had anything to say.

Phil and Cap Bozeman, perhaps not understanding what was happening but at any rate reloaded and ready again, rattled the front planks with more slugs. Morgan joined in for a few rounds then desisted as someone out back let off a tremendous shout. This outcry was so unexpected that even Barker and Bozeman stopped shooting. On the north side of the roadway, above the shack, there wasn't a sound, but suddenly down southward some distance from the shack, several Springfield carbines, Army Issue, exploded. They had the roar and backlash of a buffalo gun. For all the fact that they were very short, very elemental weapons, they threw a bullet nearly the size of a man's thumbnail, which tumbled end over end in the air, making a terrible wound when they ripped into something.

That howling man out back suddenly stopped in mid-breath. The Springfields, being single-shot weapons, were alternating; two troopers firing while two reloaded. Anyone who'd ever heard that kind of volley-firing by relays, and who'd heard the unmistakable, coughing roar of Springfield carbines, knew soldiers were behind them.

Inside the shack, towards the rear wall, a man was howling for someone to get back. He roared that over and over again in a powerful, youthful voice, until someone yelling in a deeper, scratchier tone told him to shut up; whoever he was yelling at wasn't coming back.

Out of all this Murph and Morgan guessed what'd happened around there. Someone had tried breaking away through that back door and fleeing southward, but those soldiers, alerted by Murphy's two shots, were watching. They'd caught that fleeing man with their Springfields, cutting him to pieces at that close range.

Now, as the wild yelling and shooting diminished down to a breathless silence, Captain Hunt called over to the shack. 'You men in there: You just lost one of your companions. I'm going to allow you five minutes more, then we're all going to systematically sluice that old shack at belly-level, and keep right on firing until none of you are left alive in there.' Hunt paused to let that grisly-promise soak in before going on, offering Peterson and his two living companions their choice. 'Walk out of there without your guns; go fifty feet in front of the shack and stop; raise your arms and keep them raised.' Another pause. 'It's up to you. You have five minutes.'

Murph and Morgan exchanged a look. Morgan said, 'He means it. I've heard officers sound off like that before. He doesn't particularly want those outlaws alive.'

155

Movement through the rearward brush made Murphy whirl. Phil and Cap signalled with their carbines. They were coming on up closer. There was no further need for them to remain down across the road anyway. There wasn't a chance in the world for the outlaws, if they dashed forth, to even reach the road let alone the far side of it.

Phil and Cap eased down in the brush looking like a pair of ragged tramps. Phil said, 'Those fellers got a tough row to hoe. The Army don't mess around. Even if they surrender I wouldn't want to be in their boots at all. If they don't surrender . . .' Phil made a bitter grimace without finishing it.

Morgan wasn't sympathetic. 'They got themselves into it. Every time I do something stupid I have to pay Maybe a preacher'd shed tears over them but I sure can't.'

'They're smarter than the mill-run of outlaws,' mused Murph, watching the shack, thinking that five minutes had to be just about up. 'That older one took me to camp like I was a green kid.'

Captain Hunt sang out crisply. 'Time's up in there. What's your pleasure?'

His answer was a gunshot aimed straight at the sound of his voice. Hunt called quietly over that sound for his men to volley-fire. He opened up with his sidearm, aiming straight into the wooden wall at belt-height.

Morgan turned forward and also began firing. Phil and Cap followed that example. Murph took the front wall, which was better aligned for him, and threw lead into the shack from both windows and the doorless doorway-opening. For ten seconds the fight raged unabated, then a man appeared in the doorway looking out throwing lead northward towards the civilians. He fired with his left hand. His right hand was across his middle with a dark stain spreading from beneath it.

156

Bullets from both directions hit him, turning him away from the opening, knocking him farther out into the soft-lighted yard where he jerked and stumbled, fired two last shots straight into the ground, then fell.

The soldiers methodically, calmly, continued whittling down the walls of rotten planking. Murph's men were hammering at the building from the opposite side. Inside, two guns flashed and moved and flashed again, sometimes from windows, sometimes from farther back near one doorway or the other. There was no way out for Peterson and his remaining companion. They'd made their choice and until they cried for quarter they weren't going to get it.

Then only one gun was still sporadically firing from inside the shack. Murph, reloading his forty-five, looked up when he detected just one gun still firing from in there. Morgan also lowered his carbine to look and listen. Gradually Phil and Cap also stopped firing.

Hunt's troopers were still systematically probing with big lead slugs for that sole survivor in there. They never even slackened their relaying gunfire. Broken boards lay on the ground. Splintered parts of sills and jambs hung as though by threads. The shack was like a sieve.

Murph yelled as loudly as he could. 'Hold it, Captain! Hold off! That's enough!'

Hunt's men fired another couple of rounds then abruptly ceased firing. Murph stood up, big and wide and broad. As he stepped forward away from the blue-gums and underbrush Morgan called sharply.

'He's still got a gun in there! He's still alive!'

Murph walked almost to the south-east corner of the ruined building before he spoke, not even raising his voice. 'Peterson; come on out. You get no choice this time. Come out right now or I'm comin' in after you.'

'I'm coming,' said a husky, ragged voice. 'No gun, Sheriff. I'm—coming . . .'

Murph stepped sideways to have a segment of the building in front, raised his sixgun and waited. Peterson came through into the dusky moonlight with both hands empty. His hat was gone and he walked with a peculiar stiffness, as though he were fatally hit or numb with shock and disbelief.

Men began inching forward. Two troopers headed for the rear of the shack. Two more, and Gerald Hunt, came directly towards the sole survivor of that vicious fight. Peterson lifted his face to Murphy Crail. He said, 'You were a better man than I thought, Sheriff ... The damned money is inside on the floor ... We were dividing it after supper when you come...'

Peterson's legs failed. He dropped to the ground without a sound. Morgan bent down and flopped him over. They all bent to peer closer. Morgan, straightening up slowly, said, 'Good Lord; he's got at least five bullets in him. He's dead.'

The others were also dead. Captain Hunt went inside with his two men and dragged out the other one, laid him beside Peterson and returned to the shack. Eventually, they had all four of those dead outlaws side by side in the yard. Captain Hunt had the money. Most of it was still in those same little soft doeskin bags. He put it on the ground near the corpses with obvious distaste and said, 'Sergeant; fetch the horses. We'll camp out back where that spring seems to be. In the morning we'll bury these men, bring down the rest of the detachment, and head back to the ship.'

Murph, Cap, Phil and Morgan went back for their horses too. There was nothing said. They reloaded their weapons as they strolled through the cooling night. Phil Barker spoke, finally, as they were getting their animals to start back. 'A man's life sure ought to be worth more than twenty-five hundred dollars.' No one disputed that.

When they got back, Captain Hunt met Murph and

extended his hand. 'Sheriff; I'm obliged to you. So is the federal government. You'll get the reward if those men are wanted, and you'll also get the reward for recovering the money.'

Murph was disinterestedly agreeable. He said, 'Thanks, Captain. But there's one thing you could do for me I'd like even better, if you would.'

'Name it, Sheriff.'

'That ship-captain who brought your detachment up here; the cowmen up around the Bald Hills are up against it for a way to get their beef taken to market. Could you get him to line up some more vessels and stand-by down at Mattole's wharf, so my ranchers could drive their animals down there to be shipped to where the demand for beef is?'

Captain Hunt smiled. 'You can depend on it, Sheriff. I'll see it the moment I get back to San Francisco. As a matter of fact I heard General Shields complaining only a week or so ago that unless we could get more beef at Fort Shafter he was going to have to recommend to the War Department we be allowed to start raising our own.'

Murph nodded, but Cap and Phil beamed. Morgan Forrest made a cigarette, strolled over to his horse and began hauling up on the cinchas. He had the horse turned when Murph came over to ask where he was going.

'I don't know,' Morgan candidly answered, looking Murph straight in the eye. 'Maybe back to Montana, although after two years it won't have much for me any more.' Morgan inhaled, exhaled, then said. 'I'm free, aren't I?'

'Sure,' murmured Murph. 'Listen, Morgan; why don't you think over what I told you about Phil Barker's proposition about running cattle on shares?'

Morgan glanced over where Phil and Cap were talking

159

together. 'He hasn't mentioned it to me, Sheriff. Maybe it'd be better if I just—'

'Phil!' bawled Murph. 'Get over here!'

Barker came, looking perplexed. 'What you mad about?' he asked.

'Your blindness for one thing,' growled Murph, and pointed at Morgan. 'Here's exactly the man to run cattle on shares with you in the Bald Hills, and there you stand, jawing like a damned old granny with Cap, instead of tending to business.'

Phil looked slightly nonplussed. He swung towards Morgan. 'Would you be interested?' he asked. 'Hell; I'm sorry, Morgan. It just never occurred to me, what with all the fightin' and all.'

'I'd be interested,' said Morgan quietly.

Phil's grey eyes brightened at once. He reached for Morgan's arm. 'Well hell,' he said quickly, shoving the reins to Morgan's horse at Murph. 'Come on over here and let's just sit and talk. By golly; you're exactly what I've been needin' ever since . . .'

Murph saw Cap Bozeman looking at him in an amused way. Murph dropped one eyelid at Cap and Bozeman returned the wink. Then Murph loosened the cinchas on Morgan's horse and tied the animal to a shaggy blue-gum tree.